CHRISTMAS WRAPPING

BOOK TWO OF MISTLETOE FAILS SERIES
S.L. SIMMONS

Mistletoe Fails Series

CONTENTS

For Content & Trigger Warnings

and

Genre/Trope Listing

visit

www.slsimmonswordsmith.com

INSPIRATION

Christmas Wrapping by The Waitresses (1981) is my inspiration for this book and due to copyrighting laws, I cannot place the lyrics that go with each chapter as I would have liked but did try to name the chapters so that you, the reader, know which lines went with that chapter.

Mistletoe Fails Playlist

To my husband.

When you marry an author, you know the story of how you met is going into a book.

Here is ours, with a little creative licensing.

Thank Fate for playing the 'not yet' game with us, it made us who we are today.

CHAPTER ONE

Bah Humbug

Blanche

Want to hear the powers that be laugh? Tell them your plans. That is what my grandma used to tell me all the time when I told her anything in reference to my future.

I could say that this time last year, I knew what was coming. However, that would be so far from wrong it wouldn't be on the same plane. I would have to go back to the Christmas before I met Bryce to have any kind of normalcy to even dream about.

Stopping my rocker, I wait to see if Dean is going to do his jack-in-the-box impression again or stay asleep. The clock on the wall ticks away as I have sat for hours rocking him while he struggles with teething. Two in the morning is for those much younger.

Who am I kidding? I am young. Thirty-two is young. I just don't feel it. Another thing I don't feel, Christmas. I just don't feel it this year. And we aren't even at Thanksgiving yet. But I can get away without doing either as Dean is still small enough that I can skip them without feeling like I deprived my son of something.

As I place him down in his crib, hand on his belly, I wait with baited breath. Will he stay down? I have to work tomorrow

- today. With a sigh as quiet as a mouse, I sneak back to my own bed. Success.

Valentine's Day Prior

Overdue with a kid that thinks my eviction notices are a joke and what happens? The pipe under my bathroom sink bursts. Literally. No small drip to warn me of the impending torrent like Noah got. Nope. This morning, I woke to a flooded floor with soggy toilet paper seeping from under the cabinet door.

I had to move the panel on the underpinning that skirts my trailer to get to the main shut off. It took me longer to get off my knees in the mushy snow than it did to turn that knob. If only the line would have busted above the valve under the sink. That would have been too easy though.

I now have every towel, my spare set of sheets, and a blanket in the tub while the tiny stacked set of washer and dryer that came with my rental does one small load at a time. The need for an ark has passed.

Now, I can do it myself, or let the nasty man that my landlady calls a handyman take care of it. I can see that the flexible line that connects to the hard line and then the valve is all that needs to be replaced and I can do that myself. I won't have Todd in my house if I can help it. He gives me the creeps with the way he leers at me and makes comments that seem innocent but I know are not.

Breathing through a cramp, I stand with the busted line in the hand under my belly, the other on my lower back, in front of the baskets holding all the plumbing fittings. My last check showed no progress and these sporadic spasms are more of a pain in the ass than anything.

"Blanche, can I help you?"

Myles. That man makes my panties damp. That voice. His smell. His height. I'm a tall girl at five nine but he makes me feel tiny. A full beard hides those luscious lips. I want to steal the hoodie I saw on the back of the chair at the counter when I came in and wrap myself in it so I can sniff it all day.

"Just need to replace this." I hold out the line and as Myles takes it from me, there is a release feeling like when you sit down to pee after holding it for too long. I look down, my fleece leggings are soaked all the way down to my winter boots. Shit, I just had to put on the ones with all the stuffing since my feet have been freezing lately. I just fucking peed myself. In front of the man that is the star of my pregnancy hormone fueled sex dreams.

Myles looks down too. Well shit, no hiding it now. "Are you okay?"

A curse of being a redhead is that when you blush, you turn a shade close to fire engine. "I'm fine. Just peed my pants, in the middle of a store, without the excuse of a sneeze. Can you help me find that so I can go home?"

Cocking his head, Myles just stands there.

"Please. I want to go home and change so I can fix the sink, have dinner, and go to bed."

"I think you need to go to the hospital."

At my stare, he shrugs his shoulders, reaches into the bin I had figured out was the right one before he walked up, grabs

3

a roll of that funny tape the video I watched said I would need, before walking up to the front of the store.

I feel like my boots are squishing as I follow him. I can't see to tie them so the laces are wrapped around the upper part of the boot, making them loose enough to step in and out of. And to let my pee run into as well it would seem.

"You got the tools you need?" Surprisingly, Myles has barcodes and a scanner instead of manual entry with this being a small town hardware that has been in his family for generations. The beeps as he rings up my total, make me flinch. A teacher doesn't make much and with me being on maternity leave, I make even less.

I nod and reach into the pocket of the cardigan I stole off my dad for my card. With a gasp, I nearly collapse as a very intense pain twists my insides. One hand around my stomach, the other gripping the counter so tight the tips of my fingers turn white, I pant through the pain.

"Blanche!" Myles vaults the counter and is in front of me in seconds. His hands hover around me, not sure where to touch, before settling on my shoulders. "I need to call nine-one-one."

Shaking my head, I breath through the pain. I can't afford a ride in an ambulance along with whatever else my insurance won't cover. With a last exhale, I stand back up. "No, I will drive myself. It isn't that far."

I don't make it to the door before I am hunched back over, hands on my thighs as I breath through another contraction. That is for sure what these are. Nothing fake or practice about them now.

Scooping me off my feet, Myles shoulders his way out his doors and has me in the front seat of his truck before I can catch my breath to complain. "Why are you so stubborn?"

Pulling my phone from the giant pockets my sweater boasts, I open my pregnancy tracker app. Selecting the timing feature, I tap the end of a contraction marker. "I'm not stubborn. I can just do this on my own."

"Call Dylan."

Realizing he isn't talking to me but his bluetooth when a ringing fills the space, I lean back in the seat and wait. If he wants me to ruin his upholstery, then fine. My car would have been more practical. Easier on gas than this tank, leather seats that I covered with extra towels and jumbo puppy pads, and has my go bag.

"Shit."

Myles jumps and looks at me with a little bit of fear in his eyes. I'd laugh if I wasn't poised for another contraction. "What? Do I need to drive faster? Call someone? Nine-one-one?"

"My hospital bag is in my car. I'm going to need it." I tap the button on my phone for a contraction start and pant.

"Um, what is going on?" comes a voice from the dash.

"Dylan, I need you to go lock up the store. Don't worry about the register or anything, just turn off the lights, set the alarms." Myles is going a little above the speed limit as we make our way close to the edge of town. The highway will take us to the new hospital that was built about fifteen minutes out. I'd tell him to slow down, but these contractions are serious and think we might need to risk a speeding ticket. I just won't tell him that. His panic is cute, I just don't want to add to it.

"Why?" you can hear the smile in the man's voice.

"Dammit Dylan, just please do it. Blanche was getting some things and her water broke." Frustration tinges his voice as he signals for the ramp that will take us to the four lane.

"If her water broke, and you are going to fix it, why didn't you just lock up before you left yourself?"

I can't help the look I shoot at Myles.

I can see him gritting his teeth, "not her water water, her water, as in going to have a baby. Who dropped you on your head? I thought you were supposed to be the smart one?"

"Ohhhh." The voice drags out the letters, "hey, I am the smart one. Passed the bar and everything. As for who dropped me? You did, you motherfucker. Out of a tree, off the garage roof, the deck of grandpa's cabin when they took the railings off to replace them, and I remember a launching off that merry-go-round they used to have on the playground."

Now that I'm in between contractions, I breathe deeply as I watch Myles's neck turn red before his beard hides it. "We were kids and you were annoying."

I huff a laugh as I rub my belly. The skin is so tight, even without the muscles trying to push out another human.

"Don't you laugh, you give that one a sibling, especially if they are boys, you are going to be hearing about things and seeing things that will make you wonder as to your sanity and theirs. As a matter of a fact, our parents don't know half the shit we did to each other." Myles scolds me as he weaves in and out of traffic.

Dylan's laugh comes from the speakers, "that's the truth. I still got dirt on him that will get him grounded or Mom's wooden spoon used on him to this day."

"Bye, Dylan. Please close the store." Myles hits the end call button on the steering wheel and turns the blinker on for the hospital ramp. "Emergency or regular entrance?"

I look over at the building coming up on our left. "Regular. Just drop me off at the doors and you can go back to work."

The truck glides into a parking spot, Myles putting it in park and turning it off without a response to my instructions. He is at my door before I can slide to the ground. What is it with men and tall trucks? "I am not dropping you off. My Mom would use more than a wooden spoon on me if she found out I just shoved you out and kept going."

I'm glad he won't listen when part way to the doors another contraction hits. Standing there, panting, I grab the hand he has wrapped around my waist.

"I've watched enough television to know that those are coming pretty quick, let's get you inside before you drop your kid in the road." Myles steers me to the doors and right up to the desk.

I give the receptionist my info, thanking the gods above that they had me pre-register the last time I was here. A chair is brought for me and I'm taken away.

Things are moving fast. I sigh in relief as they wheel the ultrasound machine out. Since he wasn't turned at the last appointment, they needed to check his position in case a natural birth wasn't going to work. The baby has turned in the last week and is more than ready to come. I adjust myself in the bed that has the back raised and focus on breathing threw pains that feel like they are ripping me two.

There is a knock and the little nurse that helped me change into a gown pokes her head in. "There is someone here, he has your bag it looks like."

I'm breathing through what feels like endless contractions as they prep the room for my little man's entrance. Blowing out as the pain lets up, I nod at her. "That is fine. It is probably Myles. I told him about the bag on the way here but we took his truck and it was in my car."

She must take it as I want him in the room as she throws the door wide, grabbing Myles and jerking him in as he tries to hand the bag off to her. For a little thing, she is strong as the over six foot behemoth stumbles in.

"Sweetie, set that over there out of the way and come over here and I'll show you what to do." My other nurse is a man with the best southern accent I have ever heard. His nails and lashes are better than any woman's I've seen in a long time.

Myles sets the bag where he was directed and comes closer, careful to not step to where he might accidentally see something that could scar him for life. I am covered at the moment with a sheet, but five minutes earlier I was spread out like a frog on a dissection tray as I was checked to see how I was progressing. "Um, I'll just go. I went back for your bag, they gave me your keys and phone earlier, I put them in the front pocket, I didn't open it."

He sounds so cute with his embarrassment. I go to tell him thanks as a huge contraction hits. My vision tunnels as I focus, but this feels different. "I think I need to push."

The nurse jumps from looking over the monitor tapes, tosses the sheet off me, and pulls my legs apart. "Oh, I see lots of hair. This little one isn't going to wait. We had to page the doctor, he went home for some reason right after we admitted you. But don't you worry sugar, Kat and I have got you. We're experts at this. Been bringing babies into this world... Well, we will just leave the number of years off there so you don't judge us for being old."

My other nurse comes back in as the one at my feet hits the call button. "Beau? Oh, let's get you in position, how do you want to do this?"

I love the no nonsense of this pair and that they are listening to what I want. The doctor kind of blew me off when I brought up my birth plan and alternate positions to birth in when he breezed in earlier. Doesn't help that he is old enough to have delivered Methuselah. "I want to try on my side and maybe squatting?"

As I'm helped onto my left, I look up at the person on that side of the bed. Myles is frozen in place. Eyes on my big belly as it ripples on full display as the sheet is now tossed to the side. "Myles?"

He snaps his gaze to mine. The man has eyes of the prettiest shade of blue with eyelashes any woman would kill for, or if homicide isn't your thing, pay for. Why do men have the best lashes?

"You can go. You don't have to stay. I can do this."

Clicking her tongue at that, Kat starts moving my body and the bedding into position. "Dad can leave if he needs to but he might not want to miss this moment."

I go to tell her he isn't the father when another big contraction hits. She reaches across me, grabs Myles's hand from where it is locked on the rail and has him hold up the leg she was moving to support. All my bits are on display now.

The lizard part of my brain doesn't care. It wants this kid out now. I grab the rail on the side of the bed and use it as resistance to help push. Relieved of her leg holding duties, Kat begins spreading out the things they will need on the lower part of the bed. Sitting next to my knee, Beau looks up at me from where he was watching my son's head slowly emerge. "Ok, one big push, then we will pause, I'll give this little man a quick check and then you can finish."

Nodding, I take a deep breath as I feel the build up.

"You got this, you get to meet your baby when this is all done."

Those quiet words have me opening my eyes. Myles smiles at me, his white teeth flashing from his beard has me giving him a short nod. I feel a hand cover mine on the bars, warm and so much bigger.

The nurse behind me turns from the monitor now that the tools of her trade are spread on the bed, and gives the call, "when you feel it, push."

Eyes locked with Myles's, I do as my body commands.

There is no pause as my son slips into the world in one go.

The nurses scramble to clear his airway, rubbing him vigorously with warmed receiving blankets. A small cry and I let out the breath I didn't know I was holding. I roll to my back as they place him on my chest. Tears slip down my cheeks as I look into the face of my son.

"You want to cut the cord, Dad?"

I look to where the nurse is holding out a pair of scissors to Myles and then to the man himself. Large fingers take the metal loops, and with a couple snips, severs the physical connection of myself and the babe in my arms.

With a soft smile, Myles brushes the hair from my face, tucking it behind my ear, with a kiss to my forehead, he whispers, "good job, Sweets, good job."

Stepping back so the nurses have room to work around me, he smiles again before leaving the room.

CHAPTER TWO

The Perfect Gift Was His Phone Number

Blanche

I need to go to sleep. I really do. But my brain won't shut off. Why does this happen to me? Dean is out and I need to be too or I won't make it through the day. All the kids at the school seem to be hyped up on the knowledge that Thanksgiving break is coming and Christmas right behind it. I would be joining them if I wasn't so tired.

I pick up my phone knowing that that isn't going to help. I try to eliminate screen time about two hours before bed to help my brain to do the power down thing it is currently refusing to do. But I'm desperate.

I open a thread of messages that has not been added to since New Year's. I drop my phone on my face when the first thing I see is that pic sent to me the morning after.

New Year's Eve Prior

Blanche

Why did I come here?

I'm a month from due, I can't drink, I can't do any of the activities, I look like I swallowed a watermelon, my feet and back hurt. I could go on with this pity party or I could just drive home. Oh wait, I can't. I rode up here with Grams and Rhiannon. At least the view is pretty.

The house is massive and has those to die for windows that make up the whole front with the fireplace the only thing covering the snow frosted mountains. I am sharing a room with Rhi. Grams said it was because we are both single and ready to mingle when she gave out the room assignments. Well, Rhiannon is and from the looks of her in that bathing suit while everyone enjoys a post-skiing dip in the hot tub, she won't be for long if word gets out. Under that retro collection of suits she wears on the daily, she has a banging body. If I cheered for the other team, I'd make a play. Her quirky style and quiet air hide a deep ocean of...je n'sais quoi, and that calls to me and everyone around her.

I can't help the sigh that leaves me as everyone leaves the hot tub when Grams comes out the doors that go to her room from the decking. I'm comfortable and now have to wiggle out of the nest I've built in the corner of the sectional couch. Time for dinner if my growling stomach is any indication.

Myles

Damn!

That woman is fine.

F.I.N.E.

The word splashes across my brain just like that with capitals and periods.

That little sweater dress thing she is wearing is driving me crazy. She keeps pulling it down over her ass since the belly in the front is making it ride up when she moves and I want to see that ass. Those legging things and fuzzy boots tied up her calves has my mouth watering. The girls are all dressed up in winter fashion, but the redhead in front of me has all my attention.

An elbow knocking into my ribs has me looking to my left. Dylan just smiles knowingly with a nod to where Blanche is sitting with Keeley. "Stalker."

With an arched brow, I nod to Keeley.

"Fuck off."

I can't help the twitch of my lips into a smile I get as he walks away. Being an older sibling has its perks, even more so now that we are adults. He fucked up. He knows it and I know it and he is not going to live it down, ever.

Grams comes out of her room, followed by the ever present Rhiannon. The conversation we had this weekend plays back over in my brain. I've been deemed the de facto leader of this band of friends, I'm now privy to all thanks to Grams and her decree that it be so. She bestowed the title of co-captain of this insane train should she ever not be able to fulfill her duties on me in a ceremony resembling those cult ones in movies. Too many candles on her island, a feather coated hat, and a toast of champagne in a strange looking goblet, with glitter she ensured me was edible. The woman may drive me batty, but I cannot picture a world without her in it. She reminds me a bit of my grandmother before her passing. Fitting since they were besties as Grams told me.

I know every person here's story. The one that interests me the most is of course Blanche's. The baby does in fact belong to a Senator and not the douche canoe that brought her to town. That her father is a hell of a man and as soon as he retires this summer, will be moving here to support Blanche and the little boy she is carrying. Her mom passed away a couple years back after a battle with breast cancer. She went to school on a full scholarship due to her talent in sculpting, but ended up working in that little gallery where she met asshat to support herself, waiting until she was discovered. She took teaching classes at the urging of her dad to have a back up. And even though she isn't the famous artist she pictured, she loves her job working with the kids and helping them reach their own potential.

I know from watching her that she can be a little bit petty. Loves Keeley's sugar cookies. Is fiercely independent. Thinks you can do anything if you watch enough YouTube videos. Wants a cat but is highly allergic. And is next level loyal to people in her life that deserve it.

I might need to send Bryce a care package in whatever jail he is in as a thank you for being the twatwaffle he is. Without him, I wouldn't be in the presence of a woman that takes my breath away.

I watch as she smiles, her eyes sparkling as she opens yet another gift. A large bow is stuck to her head, she is seated on a chair decorated in all manner and shades of blue. Grams surprised Blanche with a baby shower. The room is full of laughter, the smell of some kind of cake, and littered with shredded ribbons and paper.

Blanche

When we came into the room, I felt a little bit like a shit for thinking I wanted to leave. Every surface is covered in blue bunting and tulle and crepe and balloons. Little baby dinosaurs frolic on everything. Center of it all is a throne, surrounded by so many gifts.

The food. Oh, the food. It smells so good. All my favorite pregnancy foods are spread out in a buffet for us to gorge ourselves on. A cake shaped like a pregnant belly in a cute dress of fondant, made by Keeley herself, sits next to a very large sleeping dinosaur made of diapers and baby supplies.

I wanted to cry, but I was informed, by a very proud Grams, that there was no time for that as she sat me down and handed me the first gift.

Games, which the men won the majority of strangely, and loads of food later and I have everything Little Man will need to get started. I have a hunk of the most delicious cherry almond buttercream cake with a marshmallow fondant in my hands when I notice Myles getting up from where he was seated across the room.

A hush settles on the group as he comes and squats down next to me. Damn, those thighs look as if they would split the seam of the denim they are encased in.

"So, what I got you, I couldn't bring it with me. But I didn't want you to think I didn't get you something."

I look down to the hand he is holding out to me. An envelope is pinched between his thumb and first finger. Someone takes my plate from me as I reach for what he is offering. My eyes never leave his as I turn the packet over, using touch to know where the flap is to open it. A soft smile curls up the corner of his mouth, making his beard twitch. I return it before looking down at what he gave me.

Pulling a folded piece of paper out, I glance at him again before opening it. A printed picture of a crib has me giving a soft gasp. The detail and craftsmanship leaves no doubt this is no run of the mill crib you get at a big box store. No, someone poured a whole lot of time into this.

My eyes dart to Myles's again and see the smile has faded and he looks a little worried. "Grams let me in, don't worry, I wouldn't enter your space without some kind of permission and she stayed with me the whole time."

What? I look at the picture again and notice the room the crib is in. It is the room the girls painted for me. I hung those curtains and I painted each of those cute little dino canvases that now hang in a row over the head of the crib. "Oh."

Myles reaches for the paper. "You don't like it? I can take it out and you can get something more to your taste. I..."

I jerk the picture protectively to my chest. "No. I want it. It is perfect. Don't you dare take it back."

Myles is looking at where his hand is prisoner in my boobs. His fingers twitch.

"Myles Dean Carver, we do not fondle pregnant boobs."

Myles

Grams. Damn that old bat for interrupting.

But seriously, what was I going to do? Pulling my hand from where Blanche has it smashed to her cleavage, I pat her knee and stand to return to my place. I watch as she shows the photo to everyone with a beaming look of pride on her face.

In another place, I would be seated next to her. In another time, I would have given her the crib in person. In another life, we would be celebrating the baby she carries as a couple.

I have spent so much time watching from the sidelines as she made her life here that I feel like I know everything about her. I know her dreams for her son. I know what she wishes for him. I know her fears. And I feel them like they are my own.

The waitstaff have been sneaking in and breaking down the buffet and slyly cleaning as a signal that it is time for us to wrap up this party. I clap Dylan on the shoulder as I stand. He is not far from the stalker he accused me of being when it comes to something we want, but cannot have.

The house is quiet. The fire dying in the grate in front of me is the only sound as everyone has long gone to bed. Dylan

16

was snoring so loud that I couldn't sleep, so here I am. The soft lighting on the outside of the house allows me to see the fat snowflakes as they fall. I can almost hear the silence of them.

Sounds strange, but snow isn't quiet. There is a hush to the settling of the crystalized air. A moment like a sigh, like when you touch a lover in just the right way. Some call it peace, I call it anticipation.

A stair behind me creaks. Looking at the room's reflection in the glass, I pause in taking a drink of the scotch in my hand at the recognition of the person who is coming down. I felt the weight of her being even before she headed for the kitchen. I'm slouched down in the cushions, in the pile of pillows and blankets she built earlier. She might not know I'm here if she isn't paying attention, intent on getting a drink of water if the sounds from the kitchen are anything to go by.

The clinking of silverware on dishes has me arching a brow as I watch the doorway she disappeared into, using the window like a mirror. Soft humming drifts to me. You Are My Sunshine. I can't help the smile. Mom sings that all the time and has for as long as I can remember to her own children, and every other child that enters her presence. Every cousin, cousin's cousin, and hired hand's kid has been treated like her own.

Watching Blanche's reflection as she comes from the kitchen with a glass of water and small plate with a piece of cake balanced on top, I wait for her to notice me or leave. I'm not sure which I would prefer. She must be lost in her own thoughts as she rubs her belly, humming, coming around the corner of this gigantic couch. Setting her snack on the ottoman, she leans back and nestles in.

Blanche

I know he is there. I heard Dylan snoring like he has for the last couple nights and Myles leaving the room to sleep on the

17

couch. I think Dylan is faking it though. Shortly after Myles leaves each night, the sound stops. Could be a guy thing from having to share a bed, or a brother thing and the urge to annoy a sibling. I'm not brave enough to try to catch him in the act, so I'll leave it for Myles to figure out.

"Can I have a blanket?"

Myles pulls one from the pile he has commandeered. It is the softest one of the three and extra toasty from not being on the top. Tucking it onto my lap, I grab my plate and glass.

Myles tosses off the remainder of the blankets and pads over to the fire. I watch the play of muscles as he palms the hunks of wood into the coals, shaking them to get the flames built back up. With his shirt on the ottoman, I'm treated to a show as he makes sure I'll be warm enough. A tattoo runs the length of his spine, disappearing into the flannel pants he is wearing. It looks almost like a crop circle but in a line with a geometric pattern of circles and blacked in dots. The artist in me wants to trace it, the hormonal pregnant demon on my shoulder says to do so with my tongue.

"Myles." I get a hum in response. Let's just go for it. Shoot my shot as they say. "I'm horny."

"Fuck."

Looking up from the hunk of cake on my plate, I see that he dropped a chunk of wood and just missed his bare toes. Damn, he even has sexy feet.

"Um, what?" The adorable look of confusion almost makes me giggle. Shoving another bite into my mouth, I smother it. Empty dishes on the table next to me, I stand and toss off my blanket. Padding in socked feet to where he is still crouched in front of the fire, I step right into his space.

"I. Am. Horny."

Jerking from the stupor my words induced, he takes the opening I offered. Pupils contracting, Myles takes a deep breath, hands sliding up my thighs, under the giant shirt I'm wearing to sleep in. Fingers slip under the band of my panties and drag them down my thighs. They don't even hit the ground before those fingers are back, pushing my shirt up. Beard scraping deliciously against my hip, warm lips planting kisses. Surging to his feet, my shirt is tossed to the side.

Myles scoops me up and plants me on my back in my nest which is spread over the lounge part of the couch. Wasting no time, my knees are shoved wide and his head disappears. I nearly launch off the couch when his tongue licks me from ass to clit.

HOLY FUCK!!

I try not to swear since I don't want to risk slipping in front of the students but that is all my brain is chanting as Myles eats me like a starved man. Licking, sucking, small nibbles, and tongue fucking, has me seeing stars as I come hard and fast. I never knew that having my butthole licked would feel like that. I'm not a prude, I've done anal and rimming, but having it licked...nope. And I will be wanting that done again.

Over six feet of man stands from kneeling at the end of the couch. Hands shoving those flannel pants down thick thighs. The light dusting of hair across his pecs and stomach has me damn near drooling. I knew he would be manly under those tee shirts and flannels. And not an ab in sight. Yay to me for finding a man that has a real body and rocks it. Shutting off the thoughts that pop my last two mistakes into my brain, I focus back on the man in front of me.

Eyes following that trail of hair down, I can't stop myself from licking my lips if I tried. Sitting up, I scooch to the end of the cushion and reach for a dick that makes me all Goldilocks feeling with 'it was just right'. The man has the perfect dick. Some girth but not too thick, length a little more than average. Just right.

Stroking from root to mushroom head, loving the sound it draws out of him as he lets his head fall back, eyes closing, hands clenched into fists. Licking the precum that seeps from him, I moan and suck him in.

Myles

With a jerk and hiss, I pull Blanche off my cock. Hands on either side of her head, I look into those bright blue eyes. I don't know what she just did with her mouth but I've *never* had someone do that. I felt her press and suck me to the roof of her mouth and the ridges of her palate were feeling so good and then there was this popping feeling to the head on a ridge near the back of her mouth. If she had done that anymore, I would have blown my load.

Pulling her to her feet, I motion to the couch with a nod of my head. "Arms braced on the back, knees on the edge."

With a small smile, she moves to obey. I don't want to worry about her breathing while being on her back or smashing her stomach into the couch if she is bent over. I researched sex with a pregnant woman and there are a few positions that are comfortable for them when they are this far along. I was curious about the mechanics of it when she got bigger, falling a bit down a rabbit hole when the pregnancy app I have offered an article on just that.

Kicking out of my pants that are still around my ankles, I return the smile that hasn't left her face as she looks at me over her shoulder. She bites her lip as I give myself a stroke. Bites. Her. Fucking. Lip.

Bracing one hand next to hers on the back of the couch. I kiss the smile from her lips. Tasting of the almond cherry cake she just ate, I lap into her mouth to steal the flavor. I will forever think of her when I get a cupcake from Beanery.

Moans echoing each other, I slide my other hand around her hip and between the crease of her sex. Wet slick meets me, clit engorged, I rub around the little nub.

Blanche gives a little buck into me before arching her ass and rubbing against my hard dick. Releasing the kiss, I stop rubbing her clit long enough to make sure I am notched into her opening before going back to playing with her.

With short pumps I work into her. I know I didn't give her nearly enough foreplay to be ready for me, but I cannot wait to be inside this woman finally. Soft pants fill the air to match the strokes of my dick. My balls slap my fingers when I bottom out. Fuck she feels good. Her wet heat gripping me to the point that if I'm not careful, I'll not hold out until she gets her second. And she must have another. Forehead against the back of her neck, fingers working her clit, I pull out and surge back in.

"Myles."

Blanche's whine has me picking up the pace. Biting my own lip with the hopes that the pain centers me enough I can get her to the finish line, I fight to keep the pace. I want to just pound into her but I can tell this is how it is going to work for her by the moans she is trying to smother on the couch and the way her pussy is squeezing me.

Fingers join mine and I let her take over, I let mine rest over hers so I know what she likes. When her hand moves to use my fingers like hers were, I'm elated that she is showing the exact tempo, pressure, movements, position she likes. I want her to feel as good as she is making me.

Having taught me how she likes it, she slides that hand back and grabs my balls. With a grip around them, she steers me into what she needs. I can't hold out. "Cum, for the love of fuck, cum. Cum for me, with me. Please Blanche."

21

I bite into her trapezoid. That muscle between her neck and shoulder bears the imprint of my teeth now. I want to mark her so no one else will touch what is mine. With a gasp, she does just that. Walls milking me, I give them what they want and fill her up.

Sweaty skin sticking to each other, I spoon Blanche as she naps after that workout. Her phone lays on the ottoman with mine. I didn't even notice her with it, but that makes this easier. Picking it up, I tap it awake.

No passcode, no security. Lucky for me, something she and I will have to talk about later. I see she has a family tracking app she shares with her dad and the girls. I still go into her app store and download the tracker I have the matching software for. In her settings I change the notifications and permissions so she has no idea it is there. It won't even run in the background or take up unnecessary amounts of battery. I can't have something that would do that and leave her without a way to call for help if needed.

I don't want to be like this, but her safety is a huge worry of mine. I know I can find her whenever I want with this being such a small town, but I do need this. I can kill the app anytime from my own phone if she ever tells me to fuck off. I pause as that thought blinks into being. Nope, won't be doing it even then.

Picking up my phone, I stretch out my arm. It is awkward but I'm able to place the arm under her on the mound of her stomach. Blanche's top arm is over her breasts, the palm under her cheek, bottom is now laced with my fingers over the baby. Our legs are tangled but you can't see anything but my large shoulders behind her. I place a kiss on hers and push the button to take a picture. I send it to her.

Blanche

The ding of my phone has me waking from the most peaceful sleep I have got in a long time.

Swiping the screen to my texts, I see a photo from an unknown number. Tapping it, I can't help the smile that curls my lips. Yes, we are naked but not a thing about it isn't tasteful. No nipples, vag, or peen is to be seen. I want to set it to my home screen but know better. I press up into a sitting position. I huff a little as I maneuver from Myles's arms due to my size and the fact I have to leave them.

Looking at the man laying behind me, I bypass my nightshirt and snag Myles's from where it was tossed on the footstool. "Good night, Myles, sleep tight."

"You too, Sweets, you too."

My side of the bed is cold as I slip back in.

CHAPTER THREE

Needing Some As Alone As I Can Get Time

Blanche

The sound of my alarm is jarring after the little amount of sleep I have had. Teething babies are not for the faint of heart. The bad part is he sleeps so little at night, that he takes too many naps during the day, and the daycare just lets him do it.

And diddling yourself to the memory of one of the hottest nights you've ever had might exhaust you so you can sleep, but the hours left for me to do so were too few.

Thanksgiving break is just a few days away and I am praying I can make it. I need to recharge my social batteries as well as getting some freaking sleep.

St. Patrick's Day Prior

Myles

Spring is starting to break winter's hold on our little town and the do-it yourselfers are out in abundance. Yes, Carver Hardware is doing a booming business. No, that does not make me happy.

All I want to do is run across the street. Sure, a cocoa would be nice as there is still a nip in the air. But that is not the reason I want to give up helping the newest person who just came in.

She is there. I saw her walk in as I was lifting down a watering can for Sheila. As the place is mine, sure, I can just duck out when I want. Would I do that? No. My grandfather taught me better. My mom would whoop me with her favorite spoon. When word got around, people would take their business elsewhere. It is my know-how and ability to find whatever they wanted, and my sparkling personality, that has the town's loyalty. I laugh to myself at the thought of me having a sparkling anything.

"No, I think that one is too big. I mean, once full of water, I won't be able to lift it. I mean, it isn't like I have a man to help. Unless, you would like to loan me your muscles when it comes to watering my plants. I do just love how – big – the ferns you have are." Sheila is literally batting her lashes at me.

Placing the can back on the top shelf, I step back. The giant cans are on the top for a reason. No one buys them. I got them two years ago instead of what I really ordered. "You got something in your eye? That shelf is dusty."

Sheila huffs at me, crossing her arms over her chest that is in danger of spilling out of her top. "I'm fine. Guess, I'll take one of the smaller ones to go with those seeds I laid on the counter."

The smell of her perfume follows me to the counter. Something worse than that scent the old women drown themselves in on Sunday. Flipping all the packets back side up, I quickly scan them, waiting for Sheila to bring the can up with her. It barely touches the counter before I snatch it up and scan it as well. Stuffing it all into a paper bag, I hold my hand out for payment. "Nine seventy-three."

"As soon as the weather breaks, I'll be back for some topsoil and mulch." Eyes batting those lashes that make her look like she has a spider glued to her eyelids, Sheila holds out her card. I notice her nails are painted a glaring shade of pink and come into points. They are so long there is no way she can wipe her ass.

Shuddering at the thought of those things near my junk, I snag the card and run it, turning the reader towards her for the pin.

"You want to come help. I can cook you up something special as payment." Tits nearly spilling from her neckline as she leans on the counter, Sheila takes the card and receipt, stuffing them into the very tight jeans she is wearing.

"Pass. By then the garden center will be open and I will have my own planting to do on the farm."

She may be walking out of here in a huff, but like a bad penny, will turn back up. I wait until she is getting into her car before flipping the sign that says 'be back in five' over and lock the door behind me. I'm across the road before I can second guess myself, the door handle of Beanery in my hand, the scent of the gods hits me.

My gaze zeros in on her. Sitting on that purple couch the group of them love while they coo at the baby in his carrier on the low table in front of it. Dean. She named him Dean. I can't wrap my head around it. Did she know that Dean is my middle name?

Keeley sets a to-go cup on the counter. I can smell the rich chocolate that she blends herself. No powdered crap here. "Been busy today I see."

Tearing my gaze from Blanche, who has taken Dean out of his seat and handed him to Chéri, I pick up the cup and take a sip without considering the temperature of the lava level liquid. "Fuck!"

All eyes are on me as Keeley laughs up at me. The freaking sprite of a woman is finding joy in pain.

"Here."

Back of my hand pressed to my burning mouth, I look into blue eyes that remind me of this sapphire blue ring Nana wore. Looking down at what she is holding out, I accept the chocolate muffin offered.

"Might help cool your tongue off. Are you okay?"

Nodding, I bite the top. Keeley makes the best baked goods and I have no problem telling my mom that. She'd back me up. "Thank you. Let me buy you another."

Turning back to the couch, she gives me a little wave over her shoulder, "don't worry about it. Shedding baby weight isn't as easy as they say it is."

I couldn't stop my eyes if I tried as they dropped down those curves, stopping on her hips as they sway on the way back to the couch. Turning back to the counter, I return the arched brow that Keeley gives me as I toss a five out and head back to my place.

The next day sees the DIYers staying away. Just because it is Saint Patrick's Day doesn't mean that spring is here. Snow and wind whip in from the water. The temperatures have dropped significantly to aide the refreezing of the landscape.

Spending the morning redoing the window displays, I have just about convinced myself that it has nothing to do with the standing lunch Blanche and her friends have, when I see her parking in front of Beanery. Flipping the five minute sign, I jog as quick as the slick road will allow to where Blanche is reaching into the car for Dean's seat. "Here, let me help. That damn groundhog lied about the early spring and everything is slick."

With a smile, Blanche hands over the covered carrier. "Hey Myles, you sure we aren't keeping you from work?"

"I think my boss will understand." I walk both of them quickly, but safely, into the café. Blanche's hand on my elbow makes me feel ten feet tall. Dean's slight weight in his seat is nothing I can't handle, but he is the most precious thing I've ever been given to carry.

Inside, Blanche walks over to her usual seat on the couch, pulling a knitted cap off with all that red hair tumbling down around her shoulders. Placing the baby on the table, I don't take my hand off the handle until I'm sure that he is secure. Watching as she pulls a cover off Dean, deft fingers unbuckling him. A month. That is how old he is. A month since I've gotten a good look at the little man that changed my everything. Watching a life come into the world does that to a person. He still has a head of hair that is revealed as Blanche takes off his hat. The golden colored lights that Keeley favored have the color a shade richer than his mother's.

His little cheeks have filled out and he is alert as he looks around. The app I have says he can see better than he did at birth. His eyes have settled into a lighter shade than his mother's with a wider dark ring. "Want to hold him? If you don't take him now, you won't get a chance once Chéri and Winnie get here."

A thump of something metal on metal has me looking at Keeley behind the counter. She has that brow arched again. Arms crossed over her chest, she seemed to be daring me to do it. Stepping around the table, I watch as Blanche arranges Dean in my waiting arms. The cloth she tosses over my shoulder matches his outfit, covered in shamrocks and rainbows. He is dressed like a little leprechaun. His socks even have a print or something that makes them look like those shoes with buckles. "Hey there, Little Man."

Blanche

Can ovaries spontaneously combust? This soon after giving birth at least? The sight of Myles holding Dean sure has my brain playing happy family. He sure looks good holding my son. Really good.

As Myles starts to pace in front of the fireplace with Dean, talking to him as he stares fascinated up at the man that was present when I squeezed him out of vajayjay, I move to the counter where Keeley has now been joined by Winnie and Chéri.

"What is it about a man that masculine holding something precious?" Keeley hands my lunch and cup of coffee with a shamrock in the foam to me.

Chéri fans herself with some napkins as we all move to squeeze onto the couch. Myles doesn't even notice he now has an audience as he walks and talks with Dean. "Not saying that Dean isn't the cutest damn baby in the world, but that could be a puppy, a kitten, some injured bird, a houseplant..."

Winnie gives Chéri a concerned look, "houseplant? You feeling alright?"

Chéri just shrugs, picking up her sandwich to take a big bite.

"Lumbersnacks holding babies, one of the lesser known kryptonite to womankind." Keeley chomps down on the salt and vinegar kettle cooked chips she loves. It really is a good thing she isn't seeing anyone. Her breath after eating those could peel paint.

The chicken salad on toasted Italian is one of my favorites. I taste none of it. Not the minced onion and celery seeds. Not the perfect crunch of the toast. My bag of chips lays unopened on the table next to my coffee. I can't take my eyes off the man in front of us.

Since I moved here, I have watched Myles. Meeting him before anyone else put blinders up to anyone that may have been a contender for my attention. There were several that could have fit the bill. Logan and Dylan are hot as fuck. Chief Dodd is smoking in a silver fox way if you like an older man. You can't throw a rock in this place without hitting someone attractive. Not just men either. Must be all that fresh, sea air.

Myles stops as Dean's face gives a little crumple. We all pause as we wait to see what is going to happen. With a little jiggle, Myles has him on his shoulder and starts rubbing his back, giving him a little shush, "you just let it out, even men need a cry now and then. Reason we hit our thumbs with hammers, gives us an excuse."

Exchanging looks with the other women on the couch, it seems it is unanimous that the council has voted that all present ovaries are now screaming.

"I still owe you for that muffin yesterday." The gruff timber of his voice breaks the trance he has woven over the room.

Mouth open in preparation for a bite, hand reaching for a drink, napkin tucked into cleavage, finger being licked from a drip. We have all frozen in place at being caught watching.

Chuckling, Myles tilts his head back to check Dean. Fast asleep, he knows he is secure on that mountain of a shoulder.

The chime on the door with a gust of icy wind, signals a newcomer. "Hand him over sasquatch. It is my turn."

31

Grams sweeps in and plucks Dean off Myles without a pause while Rhiannon picks up the coat that was discarded on a table as she follows in her wake.

Myles tucks the spit cloth onto Gram's shoulder, kisses the top of her head and walks out the door.

"You better grab that man up before that horrible Sheila Parker finally wears him down."

Heads snap from watching a hellacious ass, thank you Wrangler, to where Gram is dancing gently with Dean in front of the fireplace.

"And how am I to do that?" I know that she is referring to me and not Winnie or any of the other single women in the room. She seems to have us all figured out, whether it is what we need or want. I think she might just be a little psychic. And psychotic if some of her past shenanigans are indication.

The smile that Gram bestows on us makes me second guess what she is going to say before it ever leaves her mouth, reinforcing the psychotic thought I just had. "Leave it to me. Rhi, give Blanche Myles's number, his cell, not the store. She is going to need it."

Nobody knows the trouble I've seen, nobody knows but Jesus that Myles and I bumped uglies and I might already have his number, even if I have no intention of using it. Maybe I shouldn't be singing hymns in my head in reference to sex.

CHAPTER FOUR

Those Pretty Calendar Pictures Lie

Blanche

Glitter. The bane of any art teacher's existence but also a must have staple that you buy in bulk right along with crayons and glue. I have been informed by the custodial staff that they will not be entering my little domain until I have cleaned up as much of the fairy farts as possible.

But is it ever truly gone? Strict supervision with the metallic sparkles I'm sure Satan himself created still results in it everywhere. EVERYWHERE.

Shutting off the vacuum that is literally assigned to me with 'art room only - do not use anywhere else' written on it in big bold letters, I look around the space. A week and a half off for Thanksgiving is not going to be enough to prepare me for the next wave of holiday inspired crafts for the lower grades when we return.

Room returned to order, I shut the door behind me as I'm digging in my bag. My dad has this irrational fear of a woman's purse. Says it is a portal to another dimension. Swears that there just might be something in there that could eat you if anyone other than the owner of the satchel attempts to remove items. I find my keys in the bottom. Along with the paper Rhiannon gave me with Myles's number, I leave it where it is. I have no intention of using it after the way my interactions with him this last year seem to be – hookup-ish? Is that a word? It is now. I pause at the main doors at the sight that greets me.

The kids were talking about the snow when it started right after breakfast. I wasn't able to see it from the windows in my room due to the tissue paper stained glass mural myself and the sixth graders had done. Looking down at the little ankle boots I picked to wear, I can't help the sigh that leaves me.

Hitching the strap of my bag higher on my shoulder, I walk out into the crisp air. Staff parking is around the corner between the street and playground. Our cars are a line of defense between the kids and the traffic should an accident occur when they are outside. As I make my way down the line, I see that whoever they hire to plow has done so but the cars are all covered in the inches of snow that are now inside my shoes.

Mentally preparing for cleaning the heavy wet mass off, I take a moment to ponder if I put the scraper in. Shit, I don't think I did. I think it is still leaning up against the wall on my porch, next to my door. Dad had reminded me of it last night when he called to make sure I was bringing the pumpkin cream pie he loves to the dinner Grams is hosting tomorrow.

I love that he lives here now. I don't have to worry so much about him being lonely. But as a retired man who is used to having his days filled with running his own automotive shop, he might be driving me a little crazy.

Stopping in the snow that is mid-calf and fast soaking my shoes and pants, I stare at my car. Cocking my head, I feel the mom bun I keep my hair in on messy craft day flop over. I'm sure I look like Pepto, Dad's dog, when he hears something interesting. Pepto makes the head tilt cute with his blocky head and expressive ears, I probably look like I've misplaced my brain and need to reboot.

Every car left here has nearly a foot of snow on it. Not mine. Whoever did it even has the wipers up off the glass so they don't freeze to it. Did Dad come check on me and do this? I make a mental note to thank him since I know if I go looking for my phone, it will be in the abyss I had to hunt my keys from. I just hope I don't forget to say something.

The car is finally warm when I pull up to daycare. I hope they didn't let Dean sleep too much today, I would love to kick off this break from school with a full night of sleep. Another tooth broke through yesterday and they said he was less cranky, but still woke me twice last night.

Dean is sitting in the lap of his favorite caregiver. Melody is awesome with him. She listens to my concerns and tries to implement my choices. Unlike Carla. Carla does not care what any child's family wants. Especially me it seems. Hell, I don't think she even likes kids. The fact she runs a daycare and doesn't like children just baffles me.

Smiling to show off his now four teeth, Dean reaches for me before clapping and repeating Mama over and over. I can see Carla rolling her eyes as she cleans up the house play area, but Melody smiles as she lifts Dean so I can take him. "How was he?"

"Better. He is back to his normal nap schedule. He loves those little teether snacks you sent in." My signature gets scrawled across the end of the day book and I take the canvas bag with Dean's name on it when Melody offers it. "Here is his leftover formula and food. We have you down for no drop offs until Monday after next."

"But you will still have to pay to hold your spot. And if you need to bring him in, we need at least a day's notice. Someone might be in his place and we won't be able to take him if that happens. And you will be billed the difference of the holiday rates." Carla is such a bitch.

Melody arches a brow at my eyeroll.

"I know that Carla. Thank you for reminding me." Taking the bag from Melody, I can't help adding, "even if that makes no sense and I won't get a refund if you do fill his place for that day."

I know that you aren't supposed to leave a car running, but I am glad I did as I don't have to put Dean in a cold car. I glance up as motion catches my eye once I make sure his seat is secure. It looked like someone ducked down the alley between the bank and Beanery. I don't blame them for the shortcut with the snow and wind blowing in off the water.

Dean is getting fussy as we sit and wait for Dad to come out. He was supposed to be riding with me to hold the two pies on the passenger seat, but he still hasn't appeared. I can't leave Dean to see what is taking so long and it makes no sense to take him out as he will fuss to stay. I hate when someone does it to me, but I hit the horn with a single toot.

Dad is renting out Chéri's old place which is pretty convenient for him so he doesn't have to drive anywhere unless he wants. When he moved here, he started hanging with the old men that sit in the rockers Myles had for sale on the store porch this summer until the change in weather forced them to find another meeting place. Now he spends his days between Beanery with the same group of retirees, the library with his reading club, learning to knit from Theresa at the local souvenir shop, helping to fix the random things on the boats, or assisting Chéri when she has a big project and needs extra hands. And a cooking class that meets twice a month. Of all that, the knitting has me giggling.

His hobbies have always been varied. Mom always called him a string bean with a hollow leg. The man can eat. Reading, yes. Fixing non-car items, sure. Giving a helping hand when needed, always. He has this studious air about him. His glasses, love of cardigans, the ownership of a corduroy blazer with leather elbow patches, and most would pick professor. When people find out that he was a mechanic, it gives them pause. But the knitting. Those long graceful hands that are beaten and scared from rebuilding cars since he was fifteen, now churn out items to sell in the souvenir shop. Pepto has an assortment of sweaters and scarves he prances around town in. Dean will never want for a warm winter set. And the name of the group. Port Haven Hookers. Their logo is too damn cute with a lobster holding a crochet hook that they wear proudly on shirts.

For someone retired, he is keeping busy now that I take the time to think about it.

Dad finally comes out carrying a bowl I can see is full of something red. He made his cranberry salad. I can eat that for every meal and have. No strange ingredients like celery or raisins, just fruity deliciousness with the crunch of walnuts. Add in some whip topping and yum. "Sorry, couldn't find the cling wrap and had to wait for Grant to get out of the shower so I could get some from them, and as luck would have it, it was packed."

I let him settle the bowl and then hand him the pies I picked up when he opened the door. "I know they hope to be moved before Christmas, but I don't think this weather is going to cooperate."

Reaching for the little mirror that lets me see Dean, Dad repositions it so he can see him instead, "the plan is for everyone to meet up this weekend when the storm clears out and Grams is going to do a leftover thing to feed everyone. Myles is loaning one of his big trailers. We will get them into the new place by Sunday."

Nodding, I steer out of town to the coastal road. Logan's inn with the lighthouse and several larger homes and small cottages are spread along the beach frontage. Tony, Grant, and Chéri just signed on the most adorable house out here. "Grams said she would keep Dean while I helped out, so I'll be there as well."

Grams's place is nothing short of a mansion. The houses in town that Winnie calls 'richies' have nothing on hers. The only thing bigger on this road is the inn. It has two guest houses, one of which Rhiannon stays in. A pool with a huge patio for summer parties, four car garage, six hole golf course, and a horse stable that currently houses Logan's parade float.

A turkey inflatable nearly as tall as the house welcomes us with a sign telling us to 'gobble until we wobble'. The porch is decked out for fall, everything anchored to withstand the winds off the water. Orange lights make the rich blue of the door welcoming as we let ourselves in.

Shoes and coats litter the foyer, warmth and the most delicious smells draw us farther in. Laughter and voices drift from the dining room. The pocket doors are shoved wide so that the kitchen blends into the space. I can see into the living room as we pass, which has a football game playing on the huge television, but no one is watching.

Greetings are called out when we are noticed, Dean is liberated from my arms, the food we brought is added to the spread on the massive island in the kitchen turned buffet. "Anyone heard from Myles and Dylan?"

I freeze at the mention of Myles where I'm filling a sippy cup and Winnie elbows me.

"They are on the way. They took their mom and dad to the airport first." Logan answers around pretending to eat Dean's little hands where Keeley is holding him, making him giggle.

Myles and Dylan's parents are spending until after New Year's with their sister, Marley, in Florida. They missed their flight yesterday because Dylan forgot he was their ride when he got called into the office to take care of some last minute details with the council.

It is supposed to be recessed until after the new year unless it is a duty needed for the Christmas Festival. The members that were in Luske's pocket are giving him a hard time as he tries to navigate the mess left behind with Chief Dodd acting as mayor until the next election. It was voted that they wait until then instead of having an emergency election with a bullshit loophole that keeps everyone where they are. They know, that we know, it is a play on trying to get the shitshow that Bryce's dad had going pushed through, attempting to get what was promised to them. Greed is the downfall of many a man.

So Dylan is acting as legal representative with the support of Grams, Jordy, Augustus, and the remaining members of the council. Grams and Jordy being the elders in the community in good standing, with normally pesky bi-laws working in our favor getting to add their two cents in, keeping the scales from tipping to the point we can't get them back. .

Poor Augustus is stretched so thin with his mayoral duties and being the chief, even if Tony is helping on that front. I think the gray in his facial hair has doubled. It was another of those loopholes that placed him in this rock and hard place. He wouldn't have it any other way, the other option was a Luske lackey in the seat.

The door opens with the arrival of Myles and Dylan. Dean yells out in happiness at the sight of his favorite human. He is his mother's son after all because Myles is my favorite human too.

Myles rubs his hands together to warm them before scooping up the baby trying to squirm from Keeley's arms.

39

"Hey there, Little Man. You been keeping your momma straight?"

His deep baritone has my attention as much as my son in his arms. He looks just right there. My mind completes the picture of me snuggled up with the two of them, a little family surrounded by a larger one gathered to celebrate.

Dean babbles while showing Myles his sippy cup, turning it upside down and shaking it. He was angry when I bought it, but I got tired of the puddles all over the place.

"Tough luck there, Dean. Momma has you on restrictions when it comes to messes. I'm sure you will find something soon enough to make her want to pull out her hair." Myles rights the cup and offers it back to Dean, who just smiles and takes a big drink.

Grams walks by with a handful of napkins, rubbing Dean's back as she steps around everyone. "What his momma needs is a man for herself and a daddy for her boy."

Everyone freezes.

I'm sure I look like my eyes are bugging out of my head as I turn three shades of tomato.

Before I can say anything, Dad chimes in. "I agree. I've been looking around town since I got here and I got a list of candidates I think will fit the bill."

Death glare engaged.

Grams finishes laying the napkins and silverware at each seat with a hum of agreement. "We can compare notes after dinner, Lance. I got some ideas too."

Not one to miss an opportunity it would seem, Dean pulls his cup from his mouth and looks right at Myles, "Dadadadada."

I can't look at anyone. No eye contact. No sudden movements. I sit in my usual seat next to one end of the table so I can watch Dean in his highchair as he enjoys his first Thanksgiving. So many photos have been taken of him. His chat with a green bean. Smearing his sweet potatoes in his hair. An encounter with mashed potatoes and gravy. And the utter joy of the turkey when it was set in front of Dad for carving.

But I still can't look at any of them. I don't want to see the gloating from my dad and Grams since it was their conversation that introduced that word at that moment to my son. At the looks of 'I told you so' from the girls. They have all been hounding me to make my move since March. At the other men at the table that would fit that list my dad has. Dean hasn't stopped saying it while looking at Myles, so there is no mistaking who he is referring to. And he calls my dad Pappap, so no misunderstanding there.

I can't look at Myles. I don't want to see the horror again that flashed across his face when my son called him Dada. I know there will be pity there. I know we can't be anything more than a horny hook up that was on the downlow. I know that the pretty picture in my head of us as a perfect family will never come true. A secret he hasn't shared ensures that.

I'm pretty sure he is dating someone. Sheila has been seen going into Carver Hardware at lunch nearly daily now and he hasn't been back over since a few weeks after Saint Patrick's. What little I've seen of him over this year were quick passes with no time for talking.

Dean is flagging as he mashes his jello and pie together in an unappetizing mess on his tray. Scooping my tired baby from his seat, I make for the half bath to clean him up. His little sniffles at having been wiped down against his will have me wanting to cry too. The injustice that we can't have Myles is what has me teary eyed though, when the doorbell distracts me from making my way back to the dining room.

The man on the other side of the door looks a little familiar but I can't place him right off. Dressed in a dark trench coat, he stands smiling at me before offering his hand in greeting. "Miss Deveraux, Blanche Devereaux?"

I give him the same not amused look I have been giving people for years when they realize I have a certain comedic lady's character name thanks to my grandmother's love of the show that wore off on my mom, who just couldn't resist when she married a man with the same last name. "What can I do for you?"

The offered hand disappears into his coat, flashing the flannel lining that makes wearing it a possibility in these frigid temps, and produces a manila envelope a lot like the one I gave to Bryce. This cannot be good. "I've been sent by the offices of Turner, Polk, and Davies to serve you with papers. Have a lovely day."

The envelope he pressed into my hand hits the welcome mat and I can only stare between it and the man whistling as he walks back to his car.

"Blanche? Princess? What is it? Who was that?"

Dad comes up behind me, wrapping his arm around my shoulders. In some far off corner of my mind I note he took the cardigan I stole while pregnant back and I need to re-steal it. A single tear tracks down my cheek as I look up into the face of the one man in my life that has been a constant when all others have let me down. I know what is in that envelope. I have been dreading this moment. As soon as the name Davies passed that man's lips, I knew.

They have come for my son.

CHAPTER FIVE

Quickies & Promises

Blanche

I couldn't let him sleep in his crib. I need Dean not to be out of my sight. The Davies have come for my son. His father has come for him.

I once heard a quote that said any man can be a father, but it takes a real one to be a dad.

Well I don't have a dad for my son, yet. But I sure as shit am not going to let his father take him. After the shock wore off, I got mad. That is an understatement, I got fucking furious. Rhiannon took Dean into the room off the living room that Grams had refurbished to be every child's dream while I had a moment.

Had a moment. That is what Grams called it as she handed me no less than three fingers of whiskey. I wipe at the tear hanging on before it can drip off my nose. I'm sick of crying. Tears aren't going to do me any good. Tears won't stop them for coming for Dean.

Dylan took the papers with the promise he will do whatever he can to help us. Chéri is going to dive back into the stuff she has from her break up with Bryce to see if there is any mention of the Davies family. Winnie is going to do the same with her contacts in the media world. Grams has promised that money will not be an obstacle in fighting whatever this is. The others are here for whatever needs doing.

Dad is dad. My rock. He even gave me the sweater back. He wants me to move in with him. Said I can have his room for me and Dean and he will take the smaller room. I turned him down.

The one face I kept looking for ducked out when it was revealed what was in the envelope.

I never made it a secret who Dean's father is. Hell, the whole town knew the day I arrived thanks to Veronica and pointing out that Bryce couldn't be. Senator Christian Davies. Rumored to be on the way to the big white house that sits on Pennsylvania Avenue. I'm sure his sister is riding his coattails the whole way since she was denied that residence when her plans crashed and burned around her now incarcerated ex-fiancé.

They want a paternity test. I have to have Dean first thing Monday morning at a private clinic on the other side of the county. They are gracious enough to pay for it, no matter the outcome. Depending on the results, further actions may be warranted. Threats. It was all clear in the letter that accompanied the legal papers. Well, as clear as they could be without it biting them in the ass.

I will not be threatened. My son will not be threatened. I informed Christian of my pregnancy and the fact I was going to keep it as soon as I knew. He told me it was my choice. He also told me he wanted nothing to do with any of it. Would not be contributing anything to the welfare and upbringing of the child. Insisted I have a will drawn up that leaves custody to my dad if anything should happen to me. Made me sign papers that excused him from all his rights.

I was happy to do so. I just wanted my baby. If he wanted to be part of its life, that would have been fine too, we'd have worked something out. When that test showed two little lines, I'd done some research. The whole family is backstabbing, use you for what they can, ignore those they deem beneath them. Christian is just better at hiding it, the reason why he is sitting where he is and the rest haven't made it into the political world. And then that run in with Veronica, I didn't want my son anywhere near her for sure. Even if she is his aunt. She just solidified that I was on the right track signing all that paperwork.

They will not have my son. Over my dead body.

Spring Prior

Myles

Fucking Sheila. If that woman comes in here one more time hitting on me I'm going to break the biggest rule my grandfather taught me about this business. But being nice is no longer in my vocabulary when it comes to that woman. She touched me. And it wasn't friendly or innocent.

Full on ass grab. Hand full, with a firm squeeze. I have told her no in every nice way I can. I have ignored her comments. I have avoided her when I see her out in public if I can. I have pretended to not see or hear her too. And I have had enough.

I sent Chéri inside while I took over watering the plants in the greenhouse. I needed five minutes. I have been missing Blanche's lunch dates and the chance to see her thanks to that woman. The sound of feet on the gravel has me ducking farther into the greenery.

"Myles?"

Dropping the hose, I step back around the display of decorative shrubs and come face to face with Blanche. Today is warm and the outfit she is wearing had me leaking like the hose on the ground behind me.

Cut off shorts show those thighs I want wrapped back around my head. The thin teal short sleeved tee is see through enough I can see her bra under it. She has on those boat shoes that are popular. Her right ankle has a thin silver chain around it. Her hair is up in a high pony and I want to wrap it around my hand, smashing those glossy lips on mine just to see what flavor lip stuff she chose.

"I messaged Chéri earlier about some houseplants that are kid friendly." And the end of the tail of hair is now being wrapped around her finger as she looks around. Just like I am, even if she doesn't know it.

With a turn to hide me adjusting my dick, I look over the area designated to those plants. "We have a bit, if it has a red dot on the tag, it is poisonous in some way so stick to the green dots. Where is Dean?"

That ass encased in denim is now in my laser focus as she looks in the direction I pointed. "Dad has him over at Beanery showing him off."

She fingers the leaves of a sad looking spider plant that the hook broke on the hanging pot, causing it to hit the ground. "I have some better looking ones in the overstock if you want to have a look at them. I broke the hanger on that one, it is marked half off since I don't know it will survive being slammed to the ground on its top."

Nodding, Blanche turns and waits for me to follow her. I don't allow people in here due to the mess it generally is with all the plants, but I want a private moment with her. I point over her shoulder to the hanging pots. She turns to look at me, lips parted to say something, but just stops.

I do just as I was imagining seconds earlier. I grab that hair, wrap it in my fist and smash those lips to mine. Strawberries. Her lips taste like strawberries. With a growl, I spin her into me, crushing her to my chest.

Blanche's hands knock off my ball cap and are tangled in my hair. I love the tug she gives when I nip her lush bottom lip. My hands are on her waist, following the band of her shorts to the button. They pool at her feet along with her underwear as my fingers slip into the folds at the center of her. Wet heat has me growling again.

I rip the tee over my own head, tossing it on the stack of pallets behind her. Lifting, I set her ass just on the edge. My shoulders have her thighs pressed open as I lick into her center. Fuck, the taste of her drives me mad. I push a little on her chest and she obliges, leaning back, hands braced, opening her hips more for me.

Licking and sucking her clit has it swelling under my attention. Slipping down I make my tongue hard where I was just soft and drill it in and out of her. I can't get enough of her, but her grip on my hair tells me she wants my attention elsewhere.

Surging back up, I take her mouth once again with mine, groaning when her hands land on the fastening of my pants. Shoving the material down under my ass, Blanche wraps those long fingers around my pulsing length. Pumping to match the rhythm of my tongue, she has me worked up and leaking even more in no time.

"Please, Myles, please."

I can't resist her begging. The pallet stack she is setting on has her at the right height if I bend my knees a little and that will just give me more power to fuck her with. I let Blanche pull me to her entrance, rubbing the head into the mixture of my saliva and her own juices over her clit before notching me at the heart of her heat.

Pushing in, I capture the gasps she gives me with my kiss before pulling out just as slow. The next push has a little more power behind it and more of my length disappears. I continue with the slow push and pull until I am fully seated in her moist channel. I pause to pant into her neck.

Head falling to the side, she gives me more room and I can't resist. Nudging the collar of her shirt out of my way, I sink my teeth into her flesh once again. A sharp inhale matches the clenching of her inner walls from the pain and I began moving in earnest. The grip her pussy has on my cock gets me right there fast, but she hasn't fallen over that edge yet. Bracing a hand near her hip, I move my other to where we are connected, pressing and strumming her button has her detonating. Nails biting into my hip like my teeth in that sweet spot on her shoulder.

"Oops!"

FUCKING HELL!!

I was right there with her, ready to leave my mark inside her. I use my own body to hide Blanche as I look over my shoulder at my brother. I am going to murder him and use him as fertilizer on the farm. Mom might miss him but Pops won't when I explain why it had to be done. As a man, he'd understand. As a fellow older sibling, he'd more than understand.

Blanche pushes at my chest and reaches with her toes for the pile on the ground between my feet. Nails a metallic shade to match her shirt have me wanting to kill my brother just little bit more. Her shorts disappear from sight as I remain where I am to keep Dylan from seeing what is mine. Hands grab the waistband of my own pants and tug them back up, tucking my hard cock as best as they can back in.

"I'll... Later, maybe." Blanche flees as she pulls her shirt back into place. Her clothes are back on but very rumpled. That pony tail that had my attention limp on the back of her head. She flees past us both and out the front.

"Did I...? Was that...Blanche? Are you and her...?" He makes a hole with one fist and shoves his finger into it. How mature.

"You are a cockblocking asshat. I finally get another taste of her and you interrupt."

"Wait, another? Are you and her a thing? And keeping it a secret why?"

"We are not a thing. I want to ask her, but all that seems to be happening when I get her alone is..." I wave a hand at the area around me. "I thought I scared her off the first time when I bit her." I look down at my boots in thought. I bit her again and she responded just like the last time. But lunch would have been better than just dicking her down in my greenhouse when it comes to the long term plans I have made in my head.

Dylan cocks his head and looks me up and down. "A biter. Never pegged you for anything other than vanilla, in the dark, missionary position."

The grossed out surprise on my face is evident even with a beard on half my face, "you have thought of me having sex? Sick."

"NO! I mean I saw you that one time all over that girl in high school and thought it looked like you were trying to eat her face off. But rewind, when did you and her hook up before?"

I can't help the growl in my voice. "It wasn't a hook up."

Planting his ass on the pallet I just had Blanche wrapped around me on, he motions for me to go on. "If you aren't dating, and have only ever been with her once before, and

49

others don't know, it sounds like a hook up to me or a sneaky link."

"It wasn't either of those. Fuck, you are annoying. I don't know why I didn't drown you when we were kids."

Flipping me the bird over his shoulder, he hops off the pallet I want to take home and hang on my wall like some kind of trophy, "oh, you did. At Grandpa's cabin, remember?"

As Dylan steps out of the wall of plants, I notice someone quickly walking away. Fucking nosey ass small town people. They better not cause any trouble with whatever they overheard.

Fixing my own clothes, I walk back out into the main greenhouse only to see none other than Sheila hightailing it down the sidewalk.

Blanche

I don't stop when Chéri calls my name as I enter the store and beat feet to the restroom in the back.

I smooth my clothes in the mirror, swipe the slight smudge from under my eyes from my mascara, before just staring at the mess that is my hair.

I'm pulling the slightly stretched neck of my shirt to the side to inspect yet another bite mark when a hair brush is held in front of my face.

"Care to explain?" Meeting Chéri's eyes in the mirror, I yank the band from my hair and flip over to pull it back up. "So two men were in that greenhouse, which was it? Luscious lumbersnack? Pinstripe playboy?"

I refuse to answer her. I don't know if I can. Can I really? I don't know what we are. Just a sneaky hook up it seems and I'm not really proud of myself if that is what I'm worth. But damn is the dick good. Better than good as I have cum both times and I can't say the same for the last two men I slept with before Myles.

"Fine. Keep your secrets but I have my ways." With a sniff, Chéri turns from the bathroom door to leave. "Can I help you?"

The change in tone and topic has me looking out the open door. Sheila stands there with her hands on her hips and a nasty look on her face as she scans me from head to toe. The only thing that sets her apart from her sister Carla is the fact that Sheila has massive fake tits that are always on display. Hell, even her brother Todd looks like his sisters, but more weaselly. Is she here to tell me off for banging her boyfriend? Maybe give me the beat down I deserve for not telling him no?

"Do you need something?" Chéri's tone only grows sharper with the way Sheila is looking at me.

"Not from either of you." Spinning on her heel, the town doorknob flounces out of Carver Hardware.

CHAPTER SIX

Sunburns Suck Ass

Blanche

My life is on hold until the results of the paternity test come back. Even the might of the Davies family couldn't put a rush on them. I laughed when the agent that showed up to represent them during the test was shut down with the request. It isn't a matter of importance in any way, just paternity and Capital Hill if full of that.

Is Grams letting that hold me back?

Nope. She and Dad are full on with this plan to get me a man. I was informed that I was to be presentable for a dinner date at The Lobster Port with none other than Winnie's middle brother, Max. The eldest is married, and the second to oldest is seeing someone. The one after the one I'm seeing tonight is out of town, the youngest was deemed too immature. I also know for a fact that several of her cousins have been put on notice as they are on the list.

I don't want to see this list. I thought I would, but then thought more about it and decided that I would be better off surprised than looking at the faces that match the names, just waiting for them to be forced into dating me.

I pick up my phone to text Max that I changed my mind or maybe that I have amoebic dysentery when I hear the knock at my door. Heaving a sigh, looking up at the ceiling, I count to ten before standing to pick up my bag.

The man at my door is hot like most of the ones that live here. There *has* to be something in the air. Might be all the seafood making them so virile. I can't tell what his hair looks like due to the beanie on it but his eyes are a gorgeous green brown mix like the tide pools I took the kids out to sketch. His skin is a shade darker than Winnie's warm caramel tones. Fit from hours working his traps and boat, his sweater hugs his chest like those jeans hug his thighs. Like most men around here, he sports thick work boots.

Max looks over my own outfit of slacks and sweater with a ready smile. "Glad you dressed for the weather, the wind is picking up out there."

Maybe this won't be so bad. "I learned my lesson last winter about dressing warm. Should we go?"

With a wave of his hand, Max steps back onto the porch so I can shut and lock my door. Dean is at Dad's for the night but that is no reason to be lax, even in a small town. "Sorry about only taking you to The Port, Gram didn't give me much notice."

Hopping up into his truck, I set my seat belt and wait for him to jog around after shutting my door. "I'm really sorry about this. We don't have to go out if you don't want to. It is just she and my dad have it in their heads that I should be..."

Max's deep laugh fills the cab. "No need to apologize. Kyle getting married and now expecting his first kid has my mother off the backs of the rest of us. She is just as pushy as Gram about knowing what her kids need, even if she meddles from the Keys. Let's just have dinner, two people with similar traumatic parental units and a mutual connection in Winnie. No pressure, just food and company."

Returning his smile, I set back in the warm seat as we drive through town to the restaurant. "Sounds like a plan."

Friday on a winter evening, with the weather being reasonable, sees the town not going to bed when night settles in. The Lobster Port is busy, but not so much that we have to wait. Seated in front of one of the massive windows, we have a view of the dark water as it laps against the piers that hold the building from the water.

"I should have asked if you have any allergies or wanted to go somewhere else. I don't normally take dates somewhere local."

Laying the menu down in front of me, I reach to pull my glasses from my bag, "why not?"

Max looks up from picking his dinner from the laminated plastic which I'm sure he has memorized. "And she has those teacher librarian glasses. Should have known. Do they come in a kit they hand out when you graduate college?" I laugh at him, I can't help it. "Because most people like to go where their neighbors aren't sitting at the next table or to eat something that they haven't all their lives."

"So, why are we here?" I can't help the hurt I feel at thinking he isn't taking this seriously, even if I was ready to call it off right before he arrived.

Hands up in a placating gesture, "don't take that wrong. I thought maybe you wouldn't want to go far from your son. Most places are around forty-five minutes one way."

Oh, that makes sense. I really don't want to be far from Dean with all the shit his father's family is pulling. Hell, I didn't want Dad to take him to his place. I tried talking him into staying at mine, but he packed up Dean while I tried to reason with him, kissed me and headed out to a 'boys night' as he called it. "Um, thank you."

Smiling, Max points to an item on the menu in front of me. "Since you didn't say anything about allergies when I hurt your feelings, can I recommend the lobster mac 'n cheese with the new york strip? The beef comes from a local farm and is so tender you can use a fork to cut it."

The price has my eyebrows jumping. I don't expect him to pay for my meal as this night was neither of our ideas.

"Don't you dare, my momma would take a spoon to me if I let you pay for your own dinner, even if this isn't a date date."

"What is with the women here and spoons? Myles and Dylan talk about their momma using one on them all the time."

Chuckling, Max sets back to sip the water that was delivered when we were seated. "I don't know. Just seems like whenever we were in trouble, that was what was in Mom's hand."

He was right. The steak is one of the best I have ever had and the cheese is so cheesy on the noodles and huge chunks of lobster that you have to twirl it like spaghetti before you eat it. Max ordered the same but with the porterhouse. He mooed under his breath when I ordered mine medium rare. I gave him crap for getting his medium.

"Well, isn't this nice." Fucking Sheila. In the middle of winter, her fake ass tits are all but falling out of her top like normal. "Hey, Max."

Arching a brow at the tone she used to greet him, I wait to see how Max responds.

"Sheila, how's Carla?"

Sniffing, she tugs the hem of her shirt down so that the top of her bra and I swear her nipples are on display. "Fine. Been busy at her daycare. When you going to come around again. Been a bit since we've seen you."

Max wipes his mouth, lays his silverware down and gives the woman looming over our table his attention. "You won't. That is what happens when people break up. They don't come back around. And Carla and I have been done for a long time. I'd appreciate it if you'd let me and Blanche finish our meal in peace."

With a cutting look, Sheila turns her attention to me. "Find you yet another man to sleep with? You going to work your way through all the eligible bachelors? I'm sure you are aware your name is the same as a woman on TV that slept around."

Pushing up on the table, I make to stand when Max lays his hand on mine.

"That is enough. My dad always told us kids that you don't point fingers because when you do, you got three pointing back at you. You of all people have no room to talk. And even if what you are saying is true, it is none of your good god damned business what Blanche does. And I don't see her causing drama and being accused of being a homewrecker, like someone we won't mention because *my* mom raised me right."

Well hell's bells. Sheila turns a fierce shade of red and stomps off to the hostess stand. Several tables around us laugh at the setting down she just received and then return to their meals.

"Order for Sheila, crab cakes and mac." Not knowing what just went down, the hostess returns to the front with a to-go bag.

"And that is why I wouldn't date her when I broke up with her sister, knew she had crabs."

I snort the wine I just took a sip of instead of swallowing it.

"Order for Dylan. Lobster mac, salad with lite italian on the side, porterhouse." The hostess hands the meal off to the man sitting on the bench for those that have to wait to be seated.

Dylan gives me a two finger salute before collecting his meal. What does that mean? Is he going to go tell Myles? He walked into that little moment of insanity in the greenhouse and then that scene at Dad's welcome party. Does he think his brother and I are a thing? That I'm cheating? Is he on the list and knows it and that is his way of saying his turn is next?

July Prior

Blanche

Dad is here! He has said so many times in recent years that he was going to retire and then changed his mind. It wasn't until he called saying that he had sold the garage and house that I felt I could celebrate.

I could have gone back to Virginia after I served Bryce with those papers but from the moment I drove into town, it called to me and I just couldn't bring myself to leave. Chéri said the same thing happened to her. Moving away from Dad was the hardest thing I have ever done. When we lost Mom, he and I had only each other to lean on. Family and friends did the normal 'we are here if you need us', 'she is in a better place', 'we know it is hard but it will get better'. In the end, we were it. The only constant for the other as everyone else went back to their lives, oblivious that ours was shattered.

Now I have my dad with me again. No longer just able to video call, but actually see him. Wrap my arms around him when I just need a hug. Steal his cardigans. And Dean will have family.

Now I'm not saying that when Grams said she was adopting us, she was just blowing smoke. Nope, that old lady took us in and treats us like her wayward children and dotes on Dean like a real grandparent. Or that the group she took under her mighty wings are anything but a found family, but having a true blood relation here makes this feel even more like home. Like it is official.

And Dad being here is good for him too. Mom will always be in our hearts, but living in the house they spent their whole married lives in, in the town where they were both born and raised, was actually bringing him down. His therapist had been encouraging him to consider moving into a smaller home, to let the shrine he was keeping in Mom's memory go.

He was going to put him on anti-depressants if Dad's mental health didn't improve. When I would meet him after our sessions he almost always showed signs of crying. We had to have the appointments on Fridays because he would be just beat down and need the weekend to recover before being able to return to work.

The only light spot in Dad's day was my pregnancy. He was over the moon when we found out it was a boy. Was planning fishing trips and hiking. Talking of getting a classic car and restoring it with Dean when he is older. Had bought numerous shirts that said he was a grandpa in training and I saw a little onesie he must have ordered that said 'Pappap's Best Friend'.

I double check the no less than three bags and a playpen to make sure I have everything before fastening Dean into his seat. At five months, he is much heavier than when I brought him home and it takes me two trips to get him and everything in the car.

We are heading out to Logan's inn for a welcome party slash late Fourth of July celebration. Grams had wanted to host like usual but her pool had needed emergency resealing so Logan had offered up the giant gazebo down near his docks. Rhiannon sent a video to the group chat of the two arguing about string lights. Gram wanted to put them up with Logan stating that the installed lighting would be fine and not wanting to put holes in the wood. Gram won with the concession she would loop the wires and not make holes in the precious treated lumber.

Parking in the lot with everyone else, I began loading myself up with all I brought. Dean in a sling I got at the shower strapped to my chest, with the bags looped over my arms and the handles for the pack 'n play cutting into my fingers, had me feeling like a llama on the slopes of the Andes. I just step off the paved lot and onto the path that skirts the house to the water when I'm jumping not nearly as high as I can. Being loaded down as I am, I turn to the person who spoke behind me.

"I didn't mean to scare you." Myles's chuckle says he really isn't sorry.

"Are you lying in wait for me? Stalker." A quick flicker of something I can't decipher wipes the grin before it returns just as fast.

"Mom and Grams set me on watch for you. They had volun-told Dylan to do it but he and Keeley got into it. Last I saw the two, Augustus was standing between them to keep her from stabbing him with a plastic spoon and threatening to cut his heart out with it. She watches too much TV."

Wait, their mom was here? How many people had been invited? Relieved of my burden because Myles just kept taking things, and making it look like the weight of it all was no big deal, we stepped around the house. There are so many people. I thought it would be just the normal crew.

Seems Grams and Logan decided the list needed to be expanded with access to all the inn has to offer.

It seems that every close connection to anyone is here. Logan and Keeley's parents are sitting in chairs watching their daughter insult Dylan. Myles and Dylan's are with them like it is a normal occurrence, which it is. Grant's parents are manning the grills which have the most delicious smells wafting our way on the breeze. Augustus and Alice, his youngest and only daughter, are playing referee with Dylan and Keeley.

Grams is going behind Logan as he sets up the buffet, changing things. Grant and Tony are in a game of volleyball with all of Winnie's brothers and a couple cousins. Dad brought his cornhole boards and is at the top of some kind of playoff board against Rhiannon that they have going on. And there is a literal herd of dogs in all sizes throwing their own welcome rave for Pepto, who has no clue what to make of the mini weens.

Cutting my eyes up to where Myles is standing next to me, I notice he looks proud. The man is stoic and only speaks when needed, but these are his people and they are gathered in one place. I noticed when you are part of the inner circle he trusts, he worries over each of them and I think having them all here is letting him relax finally. I really wasn't far off when I called him a stalker because he keeps tabs on everything.

At lunch one day with the girls, Winnie told us that he was approached for the mayor's position in the next election but turned it down. I knew exactly why but didn't say anything as the others continued to speculate as to the reason. It was just too much, it would have put the whole town on his shoulders, permanently, where it is just a weight he picks up when needed. He would have made a great mayor but it would have wore him down. He at least knows when to say no.

With little effort the bags I brought are settled, the play yard is set, Dean is liberated from his wrap and being given snuggles from everyone. I have nothing to do. Myles hands me a cold drink from the series of coolers set out, sweating in the sun and the next thing I know, dinner is being called and I'm waking from a nap in Dad's gravity chair.

"Owww." Looking down at my chest I see that I forgot one of the critical rules of being a redhead. I'm as red as the lobster tails being pulled from the grill.

"Oh, sweetie, we thought you had some blocker on. That is only going to get worse." Myles's mom, Helen, hands me a tube of green goo that was with the cooks in case of burns and I don't hesitate to smear it on.

"I forgot when I was making sure I had everything for Dean and sure he was coated. Owww." I can't help the whine as I move gingerly towards the food. Dean is asleep on Dad's shoulder so Grams is filling up a plate at his direction. I'm glad the little guy is handling the day well because holding him at this moment would be impossible.

"Blanche, want me to help you make a plate?"

Looking up from contemplating if food is worth the effort with my skin feeling two sizes too small across my chest, shoulders and arms, I meet the smile of one of Winnie's cousins. I am ashamed to say that there are so many of them, I can't remember his name. But if I want to eat, I might need some help at least loading the plate. "Um, sure."

"Cory." He provides with a smile as he doesn't wait for me to tell him what I want and just loads a bit of everything onto the plate. And plate it is. No normal paper or foam here, these are the trays you buy for serving things like fresh veggies on at big dinners with all the sections. Gram is obsessed with the everything dollar type stores.

Seated at a table that seems to have segregated themselves by gender, I move to sample a yellow looking potato salad. "You know Cory is just going to be the beginning. New single lady in town, teacher fantasies, good mom with all the snacks. You are going to have them flocking to you in droves."

Everyone at the table cracks up. I just try not to choke on the bite I just shoved into my mouth when Winnie dropped that little bomb.

"We need to do a dating pool and see who asks her out first and who gets second or more than one date. Bet we could get a hell of a pot going." Helen hands me a lobster roll slider as she adds to Winnie's statement.

The comments and jokes bounce around our table and soon the guys are shouting them over from where they are sitting. Cory shouts out a not serious invite to go out on Friday and then claims winner of the first to ask me out and wants his cut of the winnings.

After having several layers of lotions and aloe gel, I can move without too much pain. I know tomorrow will be the worst of it. Packing up my bags and breaking down the playpen, we hear a shout from out where the guys wandered to look over the sail boat Myles has for sale.

Cory is holding his hands up in front of his chest and slowly backing towards the edge of the dock as Myles advances on him. Both are talking but we can't hear what is being said. Everyone leaves off what they were doing to attempt to see what is happening. As we make our way down the lawn to the shore, we can hear them.

"And I said it wasn't funny. Don't talk about her like that."

"Myles, dude, it was a joke. Everyone makes the joke about moms having the best snacks. I didn't mean anything by. I meant actual food, nothing dirty. I love gummy snacks and fishy crackers." Cory is right on the edge of the boards now.

"I don't care how you meant it, don't talk to her, don't look at her, and you sure as fuck aren't taking her out Friday."

Before he can defend himself, Cory's arms windmill and he lands in the water with a splash.

"Myles Dean Carver. What is wrong with you?" Helen stands where the dock meets the land with her hands on her hips and a spoon sticking out of one of her fists. She was dishing up to-go platters from the leftovers and now has that feared weapon the people around her talk about so often.

"Plenty, where do you want me to start?" Dylan shouts from where he is sitting on the back of the boat.

"You shush your mouth or I can start on you and your behavior earlier with Keeley." Helen is now stomping down the dock, the men that had gathered parting like the Red Sea for her. "You do not get to make claims like that on a person and not be the one entitled to backing them up."

Myles flinches at the spoon being shook just under his nose, some kind of salad now on his cheek.

With dramatic flair, Helen points in the direction of the gazebo and Myles trudges by. There is a whap and Myles jolts forward. Not a peep is heard from the watching crowd, many with sympathetic rubs of their own behinds.

"What is wrong with you?" Apparently board shorts are no match for a wooden spoon.

Dylan coughs and raises his hand like he is waiting to be called on in class.

He almost falls off the boat when the same spoon is pointed at him threateningly. Having cowed her adult children with a loving threat I only can hope to pull off on Dean one day in the future, Helen smirks, pushing by Myles as he turns to keep his asscheeks protected, "it is a mother's prerogative to torture her children."

CHAPTER SEVEN

Countdown To New Year's

Blanche

The final page of the calendar I have in my classroom showed the prettiest of scenes. Snowy waterside cliffs of Monument Cove in the Acadia National Park. I guess that is supposed to put me in the Christmas mood, but all it does is make me thankful that it isn't holiday themed.

I have officially decided that Dean and I will not be participating in the coming season. The push for that was the packet that was delivered by the same man that showed up on Thanksgiving with a summons for a court date after the new year. The paternity test came back and told them what I knew all along. Christian is Dean's father. Now they want full custody.

Full.

According to the letter that accompanied the nearly inch thick stack of papers, I have this month to spend with Dean, who they are calling Christian Nathaniel Davies the Fourth, before I surrender him no later than noon on New Year's Day or I can attend the set hearing date if I choose to 'attempt to thwart their rights as blood relatives at providing a proper life for a Davies heir'. They are threatening me with their money and power to 'do the right thing for my son'.

And now I am not in the mood to celebrate anything. I just want to hide out in my house with my baby and hope this goes away. The hard part will be telling my family and friends about my decision. In doing so, I will have to explain why and I just want to ostrich it.

Pulling open the doors of town hall, I read the little signs that hang from the casements above the doors or plaques on the walls. I've never been in this building and am a little baffled by the layout. I thought a more square and straight line floor plan but there are stairs and hallways everywhere. What I am looking for seems to be down the hall to my left.

The outer room is empty except for legal boxes stacked around the room by case number. No secretary to greet me, not even a desk for one. Moving to the inner door with the frosted window, I knock on the glass.

"If that is Blanche, come in. Everyone else can fuck off."

He sounds like he is in a great mood. Even the thoughts in my head are heavy with sarcasm and despair. Turning the knob, I enter an even more cluttered space. More boxes fill the two long walls; a window, desk and shelves facing the door. Turning, I push until the latch clicks, noticing the filing cabinets I was wondering even existed with all the stacks.

"Sorry about that, I got my normal case load and then those fucktards on the council won't leave me alone today about the stupidest of shit. I don't give a flying fu...duck who picks the mayor's choice light set up award." I guess he just noticed the carrier in my grip. Dylan closes the file he was working on and plops it on the top of the stack teetering on the corner of his desk. "Fill me in on what is going on, last thing I heard was the paternity test."

Handing him the newest manila envelope, I sit in the only cleared chair in front of his desk, bending to take Dean from his carseat. "That was it. Last I heard from them and then that guy shows up this morning and hands me that. I'm glad

I got sick leave because there is no way I could have gone to work after getting that kind of shock."

Dylan is reading the letter with an arched brow. "Are they kidding? This isn't even lowkey threatening. It is flat out intimidation. 'It would be in your best interest to think of what this could do to you personally should you consider moving with the option to take this to court. What it could do to your family and friends. Those that are members of the community you reside in, persons with businesses that could be replaced with conglomerate stores. Consider what this will do to your son when you lose and it has to be explained to him that his mother did not consider his future. A future where the might of his paternal family could bring him so much where you can only offer him a glimpse of that richness'."

I move Dean to my lap and hand him a gummy teether, clipping the other end of a tether to his shirt so it doesn't hit the floor when he inevitably launches it. "Even my feeble little female brain got that. And not just me, but everyone I know."

Dylan's arched brow is now aimed at me. He didn't like me talking down to myself it seems.

"Sorry," ducking my head I hand Dean back the teether he tried to toss as it dangles onto my thigh, a drool spot appearing on the fabric of my jeans.

"Understood. I'm sure you read over this, what did you get from it?"

"They want Dean."

He is back to reading the papers at an incredible speed. Patting the desk to his right, he pulls a legal pad and pen his way and begins making notes without looking up from what he is reading. I can see the paper and it looks like gibberish so it must be a shorthand.

"The Fourth? Are the fu...ducking delusional?"

Snuggling Dean to me, I wait as Dylan works his way to the end.

"Ok," the stack gets set on the notepad and shoved so he has room to put his arms on the desktop, "we will start with filing for a change of venue, we want to have it here, if it gets to that. Sympathy from the judge and all that."

I can't help the spark of hope, "if?"

With a grin that tells me this man can get up to some serious shit, he sits back in his chair as if he doesn't have a care in the world. "If. And that is a big if. I'm sure they know you will talk to a lawyer. Don't know if they would think it would be me or if I'd even take you on as a client since I was the Luske family's. But there is no grounds for conflict as I worked for his father and not Bryce. Add to that I never worked on anything that shithead was in on, so there was no contact with Veronica either. Didn't know you existed until you gave the gossips something to chatter about. But I am taking you on. Do you have any cash on you?"

While I root in the pockets of the messenger bag I use for Dean's and my things, he continues.

"What they are probably hoping for is that the person you talk to or hire will be just as intimidated by them and their client as they are trying to do to you, that they will attempt to talk you into doing as they say, maybe challenge them later. We aren't waiting. We are going to file everything I can think of to put a stop to this. Did you bring the papers you told me you signed when you told Davies about the pregnancy?"

I pull a second envelope from my bag and hand it across the desk. "Those are my only copies."

Dylan immediately feeds them into a printer behind him. "No problem." He waves a hand at the room, "and contrary to what this looks like, I keep all sensitive documents locked up. All this is minutes and papers from the council, shit that is public knowledge if you know where to look and what to ask for."

In the bottom of the bag is a wadded up five dollar bill with a cough drop wrapper stuck to it. "And this? Did you want something from a vending machine?"

Glancing quickly at my hand, Dylan writes something on another paper he pulls from a desk drawer before sliding it and pen across to me, snagging the sticky bill from my hand. "Sign here and we are officially client and attorney. I can go to Beanery for a lunch latte and cookie now."

Day one of the Port Haven Christmas Festival kicks off with the tree lighting and parade. Myles brought in a nearly thirty footer for the town, setting it with a big smile on his face and a stern warning for Chéri to stay away from it.

I have a date for the opening celebration it would seem. Grams told me early this morning, before coffee, that I was to be dressed for the weather, that I was to have Dean ready too, by five-thirty.

Grant came through with tonight's victim. That is what they are. Victims to the whims of a lady that has no problem bullying them into doing what she wants. I have no clue how he made it to the list, or who or how many more might be on it. Henry is a firefighter like Grant but from the next town over, Waterbay. I was sent a picture this time with the message and I have to admit, he is cute. We are going to make quite a trio as he has hair just as red as mine and Dean's. Freckles and muscles and tattoos, oh my. If I was shopping, he would be a firm contender.

With a nod at the braid I fashioned, I put on my hat, making sure it is pulled over my ears when I hear an engine turn into the drive. Dean is dressed in an insulated bunting thing with his own knit hat Dad made him. I have a blanket too for him, just in case. Old enough to notice what is going on around him even if he won't remember, I hope that he enjoys tonight even if I'm sure I won't.

Those damn papers are nagging at me. I'm glad it is a Friday. I took another day off, I just couldn't make my brain function. I now have the weekend to work out a plan. The one at the top of my list is taking Dean and Dad and Pepto and just hightailing it out of here. I might not be stupid enough to do it, but it is tabled as plan B.

Henry knocks and I open the door to him holding out a bunch of white roses and red poinsettias. "Chéri said they are your favorite when she found out we were going out. I'm not above mentioning I got help to impress you or that I bought them locally from the greenhouse she works in."

I can't help smiling as I take them. "Thank you. This is Dean. Could you keep an eye on him while I put them in the kitchen?"

A small voice has me pausing and turning back to the door. Hiding behind the long legs of the man in the door is a little girl with the same red hair as his but in two braids to my one. "Daddy, can I see the baby?"

This man is racking up the points. Damn you, Grams. Setting the arrangement on the counter, I pick up the bag with tonight's essentials before taking a deep breath to steel myself from the attention this is going to bring on us.

Sheila wasn't scared off and has been even worse. I got pulled into the principal's office with the head of the board of education due to her malicious gossip and had to tell them about Dean's parentage and that I am in fact not sleeping around. The minute I told them about Grams's plan and list, they let it all go. Apparently, everyone has had a run in with her and her schemes.

Turning back to the door, I see Dean on Henry's hip and his daughter's hand in his free one. "Zoey's seat is a pain to move, I put in one we keep at the station as extras when Grant told me about Dean. I hope you don't mind. I know how hard it can be to move just the base they click into."

Points. This man is rolling in them. If it wasn't for a certain someone, I'd be all over this. Nodding, I pick up the blanket on the couch and follow them out of the house. "You seem to have thought of everything."

"Nope." He pops the P. "I was given a list."

Groaning, I take Dean from him while he checks Zoey's buckles. "A list? Do I want to know what was on it?"

Chuckling, Henry moves around to my side of the vehicle and opens my door when I'm done with Dean. "Time, date, approved activities, local babysitters if I didn't have one of my own, stuff like that. Zoey has been bugging me to see the parade since they sent home a flyer with her. Not sure if it is Santa, the parade, or the food she is looking forward to the most. I know your little man is too small for all that but couldn't leave him out."

"Miss Blanche, do you like funnel cake?" Zoey's sweet little voice comes from the back of the SUV.

"Sure do, are they your favorite?" Now that I am turned to see her, she is nodding.

"Daddy likes fried twinkies." She curls her nose up at the treat. "What is your favorite?"

"My friend owns this coffee shop and she makes *the* best things. My favorite is her sugar cookies." I click my belt at the pointed look from the man next to me. "I'll treat you to a hot chocolate and one of them if you want."

Zoey nods as she clasps her hands in under her chin, "can I have a funnel cake too?"

Henry gives a nod when I cut my eyes to him, "I'll have Keeley wrap the cookie up for you so you can have it later."

Parade in full swing, Zoey on Henry's shoulders, powdered sugar from her funnel cake all over her face and his beanie. Dean is in my arms, eyes big as he watches the lights and sounds in front of us. I have a belly full of corndog and curly fries. I find myself smiling. I'm having a nice time like I did with Max. Getting to know the town I call home a little more.

"Having a nice time?"

Jordy, the only other person in this town that can rival Grams in age and shenanigans, if his elf and cat inflatables are any indication, is standing next to me. "I am. How about you? Where is Tuck?"

Tuck is the biggest damn cat I have ever seen and a rival with me for the town's ginger with his shades of orange coat. I see Jordy walking him like a dog on a leash when I go over to Dad's, and at least three of those times doing it so he could crap in the neighbor's flower bed.

"You don't think I'd leave him at home, do you? He loves funnel cake but only eats it fresh." He nods down to where the cat is.

Tuck is sitting in the empty stroller, his back legs and tail out the leg holes, front feet planted on the bar across the front.

The stroller was Zoey's and Henry brought it with them to help out when he chose the type of outing. There is a look of powdered sugar glazing his whiskers.

"How are the dates going?" Jordy is stooped with age, but his mind is sharp and his ears are always tuned to the latest gossip. He runs the page that led me to find Bryce on social media and several others I've found. One is a literal gossip column since they don't have one in the newspaper.

Looking up, I see Myles coming in his grandfather's antique truck. Chéri is in the passenger side, tossing candy to the kids.

Just as luck would have it, his display is stopped so he can see us clear as day. I look at Zoey and Henry, who both smile at me before turning back to the lobster costumed actors cavorting in front of us.

Making eye contact through the windshield, I can't help the little shiver that goes down my spine.

CHAPTER EIGHT

I'll Miss This One This Year

Blanche

Myles is going to kill us both. Just straight up murder and put us through the wood chipper on the farm like they did in that movie about North Dakota. I know this for a fact because after he saw me at the parade with Henry, he has been ice cold with looks like he wants to turn me over his knee, followed by dragging me by my hair back to his cave. Any man that gets even within shouting distance gets this stare that says he would gladly murder them and not think of it later. Um, yes please. Except for the killing part.

But he hasn't made any sort of indication he wants more than a quick fuck. I need to get it through my head that he is seeing someone and move on. My heart is calling the shots still, so that isn't happening.

Dad has Dean again as I get ready to go out with Dylan this time. I've got this sick feeling in the pit of my stomach that shit is going to hit the fan. I tried calling it off but he refused both times I got him to answer the phone. Grams is ignoring my texts and calls completely, Dylan probably tipped her off that I'm having second thoughts about this date.

Hell, third and all the way to seventy-ninth.

With a hand pressed to my stomach in hopes it doesn't revolt, I open the door. Maybe if I threw up it would get me out of this. Why didn't I think of that earlier? I do an internal check. Yeah, I could throw up. I'm turning to the bathroom to make my excuse legitimate when there is a knock at the door.

Ignoring my now churning stomach, coat on, I yank open the door.

"Ready?"

Is he fucking kidding? He sounds downright giddy. Giving him my fiercest glare, I march out onto the porch.

"Those mom faces don't work on me, just ask mine. Immune, youngest child thing it seems." Trotting around the hood of his vehicle, Dylan opens my door with a flourish like a game show assistant.

He fishtails it out of my driveway and onto the paved road as I hold on to the oh shit handle above my head. Heaving a sigh, I reach out to adjust the vent blowing scalding air in my face once he is done showing off, "I've got a bad feeling about tonight."

The same chuckle I heard the day I gave birth to Dean tells me he isn't worried. "So you've been saying all day."

Festival over with, I can't help but wonder what he has planned. All I was told was to dress warm, in layers with winter boots. No sound other than the radio playing a cheerful Christmas tune, I go for nonchalant, "you talked to Myles lately?"

Dylan cuts his eyes at me before looking back at the snow covered roads. "I have. He has been a real peach to be around. Mom ran him off to the trees the other day when he got an attitude during Sunday dinner. I swear I meant nothing by it when I asked him if was done running off the men lined up to see if you are as great as you appear to be."

I rolled my eyes, of course he didn't. I love that they still have dinner once a week with their parents. The thought has me missing my mom. She was all about family time and staying connected. I can't let my mind wander that way though, the thoughts of all she will miss with Dean and any future kids and moments I have will have me bawling like a baby.

Dylan is waiting for my reply with a sly look on his face. Butthole. He knows that I'm fishing but won't take my bait. Fine, I can play his game. I got nothing to do but sit here while he takes me to god knows where. "Been in a bad mood? I wonder why?"

He snorts. And then chokes.

I smile at his exaggerated gasps as he grabs the cup in the holder between us and takes a huge drink only to wince and look as if he wants to spit it out. Swallowing with difficulty, he sets the cup back down before thumping on his chest with a fist.

"Death by nasty days old coffee. Keeley would be thrilled it was her brew that did me in." Oh, that is a topic I want to dive into. I tried calling her when Grams told me who I was going out with tonight. She of course was busy, so I had to resort to texting.

Keeley informed me in no uncertain terms that I was not stepping on her toes. That she didn't don't give a flying fuck what Dylan does as long as he doesn't hurt me. That if Dylan was on fire she wouldn't waste her two day old coffee dregs to put out. That if there was a choice between saving Dylan and cutting off her own leg, she would rock a peg. It was an interesting conversation to say the least. "Serves you right."

The dark outside the windows is cut with lights up ahead. He is taking me tubing. I haven't been on a sled since I was a kid. I might regret it tomorrow, but this might be just the thing I need to take my mind off all this drama.

79

"I will say this before we need to put on our smiling faces and pretend we like each other and what we are about to do. My brother is a stubborn twatapotamus. I'd suggest you give him time, but life isn't like that and if he hasn't made a move by now, then you might need to actually take these dates seriously. But if what I saw in the greenhouse is any indication..."

He should be dead. We should be in the ditch because I just killed him with the power of the glare I sent him. But no, he is laughing at me and making the turn for the tubing park. "It might not be a bad thing if your brother was to get rid of you."

"I got nine lives, he has tried for years to get rid of me with wishes of being the only male heir and I'm still here." Dylan jumps from the truck and comes around the hood. He opens my door as I'm zipping up my coat and adjusting my hat.

"I wish he would shit or get off the pot," I mumble into my scarf.

"Me too. I'm tired of his pouting."

That was fun. The plump tubes and sling style seats in the holes made for a smooth ride. There was a tow rope so we didn't have to climb the hill after each trip down. The whole place was a maze of vendors selling hot treats, kids looking like walking starfish in their winter gear, and people just having fun.

At one time I thought I saw that guy who keeps serving me papers but when I stopped at the bottom of the adult run, he was nowhere to be found. My mind is playing tricks on me with all the stress. I got a week until the school lets out for winter vacation and all the brain power needed for my first time keeping sugar crazed, Santa stalking children entertained paired with my personal life has me going bonkers.

I can't feel my nose or fingers. The heat from Beanery has them burning as Dylan steers me in with a hand on my shoulder. We could have got something at the park, but I want a sugar cookie.

Keeley smiles at me when I take off the knit hat I wore, ducking behind the pastry cabinet to try to hide it. I'm sure I look like I stuck my finger in a light socket but it is too warm in here to wear it and all our gear. "Usual?"

I nod and turn to see what Dylan wants.

Does the man have a real death wish? I can understand the thing with Myles as some siblings are like that. But right now he is making a mess of Keeley's shop. He has huge puddles under his boots, his coat is on the floor, and his toboggan is on her latest decorative addition; a knit, life sized moose head over the fireplace, Dad's knitting with the Hookers is really taking off. I don't know how he got it up there. From the look on his face and the way he is twirling the end of his scarf, I can bet what might end up there next.

"Dylan." Mom glares he may be immune to but not that hiss that says his ass is in trouble.

"Oh, I'll have my usual too."

Keeley looks like she wants to stab him with the coffee stirrer she is mangling. "Get. It. Down."

With a cheeky grin, Dylan wanders over to the dessert display. "Can I get one of those rocky road brownies too?"

The hiss of the milk frother hides Keeley's reply. I'm not sure I want to know what she said as she shoots daggers at Dylan over her shoulder.

The jingle of the bells has us looking to see who is coming in. A large man enters with a quick scan of the interior before stepping aside to reveal none other than Veronica, followed by an equally thick guy.

The three of us pause and watch as she walks towards us in a pristine pantsuit that belongs in a boardroom and stilettos. "Dylan, don't you know better than to date clients? Conflict of interest and all that."

Not missing a beat, "Ronnie, don't you know not to wear white after Labor day?"

The false smile fades from her lips. "Veronica," she enunciates before turning to me. "With the rumors going around about you, you would think that you would be staying at home with your son. However are you going to show you are a fit parent? Or is this how you plan on paying your lawyer?"

The insinuation is clear. Keeley starts past me and I grab her hand before she can get close to the woman looking down on all of us. My gut is telling me this is about the custody case and I need to find out what part this woman plays in it. "What do you want Veronica?"

Myles

I stop on the edge of the porch as the wicked witch of DC struts into Beanery followed by her flying monkeys. Her handlers must not have liked her diddling the help. These two are thick in a chunky way, and not near as pretty as the last two.

When I see the telltale red hair of the woman that is the lead in all my fantasies, I make my way across the road. I knew from the alerts on my phone every move she had made this evening. That she was out at Tucker's Tubes and when they were headed back. When she arrived in town and parked in front of the cafe. The sight of her looking cornered has me on high alert. Who her date is has me seeing red. I'll handle him later.

Shoving open the door, I smack into the back of one of the guards who has the nerve to growl at me. Fuck off dude, I'm protecting my woman. Dylan is spouting off per his usual self before Veronica turns on Blanche.

Oh, hell no.

"Blanche, Sweets, you ready to go home?" All eyes swivel on me.

The smart woman she is, Blanche grabs the lifeline I just threw her. "Sure, Dylan and I just got back and were grabbing something to warm up before I came over to see if you were done for the day."

Holding out my hand, I pull as her palm wraps around mine so she is flush with my side. "Thank you for taking her tubing, that job ran over and I didn't want to waste the tickets."

Dylan nods before picking up the mug Keeley has sitting on the counter with that nasty latte stuff he drinks. I can see the dick drawn in the foam from here. "No problem, when Dean is bigger we will take him. Mom and Pops will get a kick out of it."

Nodding, I turn to the door only to be stopped by Meatball One. "I think the lady has more to say."

Meatball Two doesn't look as confident as his counterpart but nods in agreement. "Miss Davies came to talk to Miss Deveraux. I think you should hear her out."

The click of heels signals Veronica coming up behind me. I pull Blanche in tighter to my side. "I think she has said enough."

"I haven't even got started. I sure didn't drive all the way here just to listen to that lackwit you are calling an attorney. I came to tell you to do the right thing. The smart thing. To just cut your losses. You know that we are going to win. We have too much pull and you know that too. When I sent the request for paternity..."

"You? It was you?" Blanche steps out of the protection of my arm and faces head on the person that is making her life hell.

Sneering at Blanche squaring up to her, Veronica crosses her arms over her chest and cocks out a bony hip. "Who else would it have been? My brother wiped his hands of you and your child before he was even born. Not considering that the heir to the Davies' was going to be raised without our influence. Without all we could provide to mold him into the man he will be."

"I can raise my son just fine without all the Davies can provide. And if you are any stick to measure your family by, do a hell of a better job at making him a man with morals and integrity than any of you will ever be able to." Blanche is shaking. If I'm livid, I can only imagine how she feels. How dare this woman call into question her parenting? Money doesn't make up for what you lack, she is proof of that.

With a toss of her head, she goes on, not aware that Dylan is holding Keeley back behind her. "What kind mother would deny her child the chance at a better life?"

I press into Blanche from behind. Projecting strength with my body shielding her back from attacks that could come from that direction. I answer for her, "a good one. It isn't about what you can give a child, it is what you do give them. Money and power isn't everything."

"It is. You will see that when we are given custody. And then there will be nothing standing in the way of my brother and his dream of the presidency." Veronica is the poster child for self-righteousness. Delusions seems to not be in her vocabulary, but is sure fills the room with every word she spouts off.

There it is. The real reason they want Dean. It has nothing to do with raising him with all the wealth they can shower him with. Nothing to do with blessing him with the power of the Davies name.

Blanche sees it too. "My son is not an accessory to making your brother a more likable candidate."

The laugh that bounces around the room is loud and so fake. "Accessory? Far from it. Even in today's age, he is a bastard child that could be the loadstone that brings Christian down. It came out once that a VP candidate's daughter had a child and wasn't married. And instead of the country embracing her for being just like them, they tarred and feathered her before chasing her back to where she came from. No, your son is the dirty little secret, the skeleton in the closet, that needs to stay hidden. And what better way to do that than to have him in our care where we can control the narrative?"

Blanche sags back into my chest, wrapping her arms around herself for protection. It hurts to think she feels the need to do that herself.

"I'll leave you to whatever this is." Veronica circles her finger to encompass everyone present before she goes to breeze by us, attempting to shoulder check Blanche. I move her out of the way and Veronica nearly falls. With a huff, she moves to Meatball One who hands her her jacket. "You have so little time with little Christian, you might want to make every minute of it instead of going out with a different man every weekend."

"Dean."

Her botox must be wearing off because her eyebrow twitches in an effort to arch at me. "We will see."

Blanch sags even farther in defeat as Veronica makes her way out and leaves in a flash of tail lights. "I need to go home.

No, I need to get Dean from Dad. We need to get out of here. I can't lose him. I..."

Dylan hands Blanche her drink. "Calm down. Don't do anything stupid. Just be normal, they might be having you followed. If it was me, I would have someone on them twenty-four seven if they weren't so out there in the media as it is."

She looks around with wide eyes as if someone is going to jump out at her like the paparazzi do to celebrities. She makes to move out of my side but I hold her firmly. She is shaking so bad right now that a stiff breeze might blow her over.

"Nope, don't go there either. You have done nothing wrong. Go home, take care of Dean, we will meet next week or after. I should know something about the petition to have it here by then." Dylan nudges the bottom of her cup to get her to drink. She looks ready to collapse, maybe the sugar will help her clear her head.

Keeley takes off her apron, tossing it on the counter. "I'll walk you to your dad's. Maybe stay the night. You two don't burn the place down, I'll be right back. Stay out of the pastry case, Dylan. Myles, help yourself to a hot chocolate."

Blanche nods and the two of them leave us to wait for Keeley's return to close up.

I watch as they cross the street before rounding on Dylan. "What the fuck?!"

He just shrugs as he reaches for the moose that is holding the ridiculous neon orange toboggan he got from the state park the year they tried promoting winter hiking. "You snooze, you lose."

"Are you five? I told you, hands off." I'm blocking the front door so he turns to the back.

He flings his scarf around his neck with the theatrics that are all Dylan. "Now who is acting like a child? You can't call dibs and then not claim her. She will move on and you are going to be left behind to watch her make happy family with someone else."

"I'm..."

"You aren't doing shit. She thinks she is nothing but a good time. A fun fuck when it is convenient for you." Dylan is mad. Rarely does he look anything other than smug and it sets me back.

"Did she say that? I never... She isn't... I just..." He stops me again with the old 'talk to the hand' move.

"She didn't have to. You can see it. Waiting for something, anything, a sign from you. But are you doing any of that? No. You're just sitting on your thumb. Grams started this to wake your ass up. I'm going to tell her to start making real dates for her. Then you can just sit and spin, I just hope you use lube or it is going to be a hard ride."

"I'm just..."

Dylan stands there with his hands on his hips waiting for me to continue. There are times I want to punch him in the face, but it is out of love. This is one of those times. I'm not ready to have this conversation with myself, let alone him.

"I'm not good enough for them."

I've never seen my baby brother speechless. He came out screaming and has never shut up. With his mouth hanging open and his arms slack at his sides, it seems I might have just broken him if this silence is any indication.

"You know I took her to the hospital when she went into labor. What you don't know about that day was that I didn't just drop her off. I was there. I watched her bring that little boy into the world. I saw the strength it took for her to do that. She even told me I could leave. I knew she didn't need me then and she doesn't need me now."

Scrubbing my hands over my face, ruffling my beard in the wrong direction before smoothing it back into place, I continued, "and then Dean called me Dada. Looked right at me and called me his person. I might have panicked a little when he did. How could he feel like I deserve that title? Do you know why?"

Dylan has at least closed his mouth when he shakes his head.

"Because I wanted them to be mine. I wanted it something fierce. There was this powerful urge to claim them. To shout it from the rooftops. But I didn't. Why? Because what do I have to offer them? Money? She doesn't want it or she would be after Davies. Love? She has all of you. What can I offer them? TELL ME!"

My shout must shock Dylan out of the stupor he was in because he jerks as if I slapped him. "You are a twatwaffle. You better get your head out of your ass before you miss your chance at the one thing in this world that would make you a better man than you already are."

I don't know what to say as he spins on his heel and marches out the backdoor. I didn't hear Keeley come in behind me, so when she speaks, I jump nearly a foot.

"Yeah, what he said."

CHAPTER NINE

I Just Need Five Minutes

Blanche

I *am* being fucking followed. And now he isn't even trying to hide. I've dubbed him Richard. The way my brain figured out to call him that is long and convoluted, probably resulting from the trauma my life is currently causing me. With the hat and trench coat, he looks like he is trying to look like what one would think a detective looks like. He should be trying to blend in, but it just makes him stand out more. Seems he has multiple roles in ruining my life than just serving me with papers I want to burn like Chéri does trees.

I'm meeting the girls for lunch like usual and plan on giving the news that I won't be attending the huge celebration tomorrow in person. I meant to do it before Christmas Eve but I just couldn't get my shit together and it is now or never.

Richard is right across the street, a big camera pointed my way, as I stepped out of my car where I parked it next to Chéri's in the hardware lot. With a sigh, I walk into the greenhouse turned pine forest with all the greenery around, glad the main door is closed today. It feels a little like stepping into Narnia it is so lush and I take a moment to just breathe. The smell of all that pine is revitalizing.

Startling at the volume level of the voice in the center of the dome, I go in search of Chéri. "If you don't change that damn song, I'm going to stick the speaker up your ass."

The bloop of the button release on the walkie talkie in her hand signals she is finished for the moment. I stand on the other side of the pallet turned counter from her and pause to listen to what is playing. I'm The Happiest Christmas Tree by Nat King Cole chirps away in the background. "What is your issue with happy trees?"

Chéri glares at me over her bottle of water. "I have no problem with happy trees. In fact, I love them. Haven't had any 'happy trees' since I started dating a certain cop, but that is beside the point. The issue I have with this happy tree is that it has been playing on repeat. For. The. Last. Three. DAYS!"

Both my eyebrows shoot up. Myles isn't usually one for annoying people since they annoy him to the extent that he would hole up on his farm if he had someone to run this end of the business. So it makes me wonder, "what did you do?"

Chéri tries to act innocent as she puts on her puffy coat.

"Chéri, what did you do? Did Keeley help?" I can see them turning their evil brains on Myles just out of boredom. After what they did to Bryce, it couldn't be a good thing if those two got an idea in their heads.

Chéri shoves me out of the door I'm now blocking and hangs a sign on the roll up door that steers people into the store itself if they need help. "He had it coming."

Richard smiles this time as he takes my picture as we dart across the slushy road. We aren't as fast as we should be since we are bundled up good from the wind cutting in from the water like normal. He takes several shots before Chéri sees him, flipping him off before I can stop her. Ignoring him, I open the door and this time, I'm the one doing the shoving. "Don't. Don't give them any fuel for the fire. Please. I wanted Dylan to put a stop to it. He said that if we sent them any kind of desist motion, it could be seen as an admission of guilt or I had something to hide."

We stop in the middle of Beanery and stare at the sight before us.

Keeley is wearing a knit stocking cap in green and white stripes while she dances with Dean on her hip. My dad is doing some kind of break dancing moves, popping his arms and general self to the laughter of my son. Blaring at just under too loud to conduct business is Crowder's Elf Song.

"Um, Keels, what is going on?"

Winnie calls from behind the counter where she is making our lunches, "Myles got her too and she was scaring the kids, so Lance told her to embrace it. Now, she isn't scaring babies at least. When the customers see her dance moves, that might be another story."

We look to where Dean clings to Keeley, smile huge and laughter ringing out as she drops it down and springs back up with him. Moving to join in, Chéri and I bust out our best moves. Grams slides in as she comes into the store, twerking as Rhiannon helps set out the food and drinks that Winnie is handing to her.

Dance party on a weekday. The best thing in the world to break you out of the holiday glums it seems. Who cares if Richard is now videoing through the window our ridiculousness? My son is happy and so am I.

We have worked up an appetite when the music lowers in volume but keeps playing in the background. Keeley is humming as she shovels in a chipotle flavored kettle cooked chip. At least it isn't her normal flavor of salt and vinegar. "What did you two do to Myles?"

Keeley flashes three fingers, wiggling them, as she chews the giant bite of a chicken salad sandwich. "Winnie helped."

"Hey!" Winnie's affront is garbled with the size of the bite she just shoved into her mouth. Swallowing with effort before defending herself, "I only gave you the confetti."

Dad sets his cup of soda down after a healthy slurp, "accessory to the crime."

Grams nods along to the beat of the song, "yup. Like if you provide the car, knowing they are going to run down a douchenozzle with it, makes you an accessory."

Everyone looks at the little woman licking mayo off her fingers with varying levels of concern. Dad speaks for all of us, "um, that was an oddly specific example."

Shrugging, Grams steals one of Dad's dill pickle flavored chips before spitting it into a napkin and wiping her tongue with another. "Popped into my head seeing as the dick that has been taking pictures almost got run over by Myles just now crossing the road."

Sure enough, Richard is being cussed out by Myles as he hangs out his window. Looks like the peeping tom decided to take a break from the weather when we settled down to eat and was heading to his own car without watching where he was going. It must be the best he can do and keep an eye on me. Word got around in no time and no one would speak to the private dick or allow him to darken their doors, so he isn't welcome somewhere warm to stalk me from. I thanked Dylan for it, but it was Chief Dodd. I made him one of my pumpkin cream pies.

Dad points a finger at Chéri, "what did you do to Myles?" He should have been a teacher with that look. He drags us back to the topic.

Chéri ducks her head, "he had it coming."

Her latest obsession is the movie Chicago and it is now showing up in the way she talks. I swear she is humming the

Cell Block Tango constantly. I'd fear for Grant and Tony if I didn't know she loved them both to pieces. I stuff my trash into my chip bag before asking, "how?"

Keeley sits up from where she is laying back on the rug, "he wanted her to wear an elf outfit."

I can't help the snort that comes out.

Chéri turns her glare on me. "It is insulting to think that because short people are well, short, that we should wear elf costumes."

Keeley is nodding with her. Both are tiny little sprites of people in height so it is logical that they would ban together to right the injustice. "Elf prejudices."

Everyone cracks up.

Dad passes me Dean. He has been nestled in his lap while we all ate, eating his own finger food lunch as it is held for him. "I saw Myles himself wearing a Santa hat, it is only fair he asked you to add to the ambiance of the season. Was it something embarrassing?"

"It didn't have to be, he was height profiling."

The room erupts in laughter again. Seems these two have their arguments laid out.

Grams, who is no taller than Chéri and Keeley, lifts her foot and drapes her calf on the corner of the low table. She is wearing curly toe shoes that do resemble something you would see on an elf.

Even the two who are trying their best to justify their actions laugh this time.

"So what did you do with the confetti?" Rhiannon asks from where she is snuggled in the corner of the couch with her giant cup of soup. It is strange to hear her speak up, but we are no longer stopping to gape at her when she does.

Keeley starts fiddling with her phone as Chéri giggles and points at her. The screen of the television behind us changes from the weather app and to the phone as Keeley navigates to her social media for the café. You can see Myles getting into his truck and as soon as he starts it, the inside turns into a real life snow globe as stuff blows out of his vents.

No one holds back as they laugh at what you can see of his face there is so much blowing around. He nearly falls as he stumbles out, the vents on full blast making it look like someone put a snow machine in his cab. Keeley and Chéri are laughing along with themselves in the video. His beard is full of the small pieces of paper in red, green, and white. He looks right at the camera before taking off at a sprint at whoever was recording. All you see is the shaking of their getaway and laughter as Myles threatens to get even if they don't come back and clean it up as the video ends.

"You put it on tiktok?" I can barely breathe and Dean is looking at me in concern as I wheeze.

"Got four point nine million views. Jordy shared it on all his accounts as well as did several others when he reposted it." Winnie is wiping her eyes on a napkin, her liner smeared.

Shaking my head, I cuddle Dean as he starts drifting off. Even if we are loud when gathered, he is so used to us that a bomb could go off and he would sleep through it. "And now you are both listening to the same song on repeat. I know how he did it in the greenhouse, but how did he get you, Keeley?"

Keeley glares out the front window at the hardware store, "he hacked my system. I turn it off and he turns it back on. Down and it goes right back up. I know every word to a song I didn't even know existed until three days ago. Yes, it is catchy but not on repeat."

Chéri huffs right along with Keeley. "It's not like I used glitter. I mean, he could look like Holly from down at The Pole House when she comes in before her shifts. There is nothing wrong with being an exotic dancer so wipe that look off your face Miss McJudgerson." She points a finger at Winnie, "more power to those who can take their clothes off with the lights on and everyone looking. I'm just saying that it might have given him that sparkling personality he is lacking lately."

Keeley agrees as she gathers up all the trash. "Crafting herpes is contagious and he would have left a trail wherever he went, so we did that favor to his customers at least. We considered it until Winnie intervened."

The amount of glitter I have in my art room has me snorting at the term she used for the mess it leaves in everyone's life. "Did you at least clean the mess?"

Chéri shakes her head as she stretches her fuzzy sock covered toes to the fireplace, "nope. It is biodegradable. I did get him a gift certificate for the auto detailer in Waterbay for Christmas."

Everyone starts moving as lunch is over and customers are coming in for their afternoon caffeine boosts. Chéri has all of us snorting before we can make it out the door with the comment she tosses out as she wraps herself up for the walk back across the street. "Can I just add that The Pole House missed an opportunity to name their place The Crab Shack?"

CHAPTER TEN

Slutty Costumes Are No Excuse

Blanche

I was a chicken shit. I'm pretty sure I had feathers growing out of my butt. I sent a group text and then shut off my phone. Dad already knew. He is the only one I've kept up to date on all that is going on and he understands. I don't want to wish things into existence, refusing to say my fears out loud, but he knows I am scared to the core of my being that my son is going to be taken away from me and this will be the last time I get to see him. His wonder at the lights and decorations. His first tries of the foods that make the holiday. His attempts at opening gifts.

At nearly eleven months old, this holiday should have been special.

Instead I'm laying here watching the snow fall out the set of windows in my bedroom. It kind of reminds me of the weekend of my baby shower with those fat flakes drifting down.

Glancing at the baby monitor screen, I see Dean sleeping in his crib. His favorite blanket and a stuffed moose Grams got him tucked in with him.

My phone lights up. I finally turned it back on and read over all the messages that came in when I informed my family that Dean and I would not be there tomorrow. Like the hero he is, Dad handled it and they left me alone shortly after. The message is the one he sends every night.

Sleep tight my Princess and kiss the Frog for me.

He has called Dean a frog after an ultrasound appointment where he moved around and kind of resembled a frog. He likes to think he is funny and say it is because we all start out as tadpoles, but I know better. He has always called me Princess, telling me not to be kissing toads when a frog is better. Dad also likes to remind me that right now, my son is a frog and it is up to me to raise him so that when the time comes and he turns into a prince, he will be the best prince that he can be since he made sure I was a proper princess.

Wiping a tear from my cheek, I thumb into my camera roll.

Halloween

Blanche

We look freaking awesome.

A month of prep and here we are. Halloween night. All the kids were hyped way before tonight's sugar rush so I just let them go as long as they didn't set fire to my classroom. The janitorial staff will probably never want to clean my room again after a whole big ass container of glitter ended up dumped on the floor. I tried my best to clean it, but it was a lost cause.

The trials of war and all that. Maybe some line about spilled milk but they might cry over the amount of sparkle that is clinging to everything.

Dad had a couple of coveralls left from his garage. I sacrificed some pillows and dyed myself green on one hand to the wrist making a slime fountain. And we look freaking awesome!

As we open the door to the first trick or treaters and make ready for the deluge of overstimulated kids, I cannot help the smile that already had my face hurting from doing it so much.

Squeals great us as the kids recognize me and who we are dressed up as. Tan jumpsuits, proton packs on our backs, Pepto looking all demon dog and Dean waddling around in a white puffy suit. The kids don't need hints to guess who we are. Even if I'm from the one movie that isn't in the timeline. But I couldn't resist with my red hair.

Dad and I decorated the yard earlier this week and it is full on mesh of all the movies that are his absolute favorite. He even has the siren sound on his phone to surprise kids and plans on chasing Pepto and Dean around. I love that man. Mom would have loved this.

I texted Keeley earlier with a picture of our outfits and asked if she would be around to give out candy at the store. I planned on taking Dean down to see her, slipping across the road to the hardware store for a peek at the man I just need to let go. Keeley said she was, but not to come just to see her as it was a madhouse. Her next text popped my balloon. Dylan is manning the candy station at the hardware store, Myles is having truck troubles and would be working on it instead of giving out candy as usual. With a sigh, I put my phone in the house and pretend I'm not disappointed.

I need to stop giving in to the urges to open up that conversation avenue. With the normal interactions, we seem to be nothing more than acquaintances within the same friend circle who just happened to bump uglies.

Dean is out. He crashed long before the last piece of candy was snatched up. Pepto with him. Dad is sitting on the steps with Grant and Tony, enjoying an evening beer. He won't have more than one with Dean here. I never saw him have more than that on occasion when I was a kid too.

Chéri is sitting next to me. She pulled off her blonde wig earlier but the trio was Angel, Buffy, and Spike. It was so funny to see the generation that knew get the joke, and others googling it as they walked off. She nudges me with her shoulder and a nod to my car.

How is it that everyone seems to know but him? Even if we don't act any differently? Haven't said anything? Hell, I haven't even told Dad about my crush.

I turn from looking at my car now parked in front of the house to the three men that are all smirking at me. Without a word, I stand, kiss Dad on the top of the head as I go by and slide in behind the wheel. I know he has Dean and I don't plan on being gone long.

Myles

The sound of tires and gravel has me looking up from under the hood of my truck. Fucking fuel pump went out on me and now I'm here instead of in town, handing out candy, hoping that I get to see Dean and Blanche. Their costumes were so cute. The picture in the group text is now saved to my phone. There was a video too. His waddle was so cute as he helped hand out candy. I wanted to be there. Pretend they were mine as they celebrated his first Halloween. But my truck had other plans.

Dylan had stopped by earlier to pick up the treats I forgot to leave at the store to hand out for me. I couldn't have the kids disappointed that Carver Hardware wouldn't be giving out their custom tree shaped rice treat bars that Mom makes every year. He had asked why I don't just replace the truck that has been breaking down more often than not lately. I didn't answer him. How was I to tell him it was because it was what I used to drive Blanche to the hospital the day Dean was born?

I've been checking my app to make sure I don't miss a notification in case she leaves her dad's but she must be staying the night. My brother calls me a stalker but I don't think I'm all that bad. Just an app and several people I can call if I need eyes on her instead of a blip on a map.

The headlights of the incoming vehicle turn off and I curse when I see who it is. How did she get past my tracking app? I just checked it a few minutes ago and it was saying she is still in town. I'll have to check it for glitches. Stepping out of her car, Blanche walks over to where I'm wiping my hands on a rag. I'm done for the night, the fuel pump replaced.

She has the top of the coveralls rolled and tied low on her hips, a white tank showing off the little bit of glow her burn turned to. Hair in that messy bun that just makes me want to grab it to hold her where I want her. Glasses.

Fuck, she has those teacher glasses. Squarish black frames that give her a stern look. Send me to the principal office Miss Devereaux. Keep me for detention. The hand sliding up my chest snaps me out of my fantasy of bending her over a desk and hiking up her skirt with her blouse torn open and a naughty red bra.

"Myles."

Hands grabbing that ass I can't keep out of my dreams, I lift. Long legs go around my hips, arms wrap around my shoulders and lips meet mine. In the door that leads off the small breezeway between the house and garage, up the stairs and into the room I have pictured this woman more times than I can count.

Placing her down on the bed, I notice the black smears on her once pristine shirt. "Off, everything while I clean up."

Not waiting to see if she obeys, I move to my bathroom and strip down. Couple pumps of that scrub that takes rust off a car bumper and a scrub brush, I make sure that I won't leave a smudge on that pale skin. At least not one that I don't mean to.

Stopping in the doorway, I see she took the command to heart as the bed is as naked as the woman lounging in the middle of the fitted sheet. She nearly glows against the dark blue background. I grab my phone and snap a picture.

One arm over her head where her hair spreads like molten fire, other over her breasts like she is a little shy. Face a soft, sultry expression as she waits for me. Legs pressed together, rubbing slowly, hips canted a little to the side giving me just a peek at that perfect ass.

Perfection made even more so because she is finally in my bed.

Blanche

I've read the term that men can prowl in many romance books and I'm seeing it in action as Myles comes towards me from the bathroom. All flexing muscle, veins popping in all the right places, and that cock standing at attention. His hands hit the bed either side of my legs and he kisses and licks his way up starting at my knees, pausing to breathe deep at the apex of my thighs before leaving a little nip on my hip bone. Chin nudging my arm out of the way. His knees hit the bed as he sucks a nipple into his hot mouth, my back arches involuntarily as pleasure explodes from the contact.

I dimmed the lights but am now a little worried that they are still too bright. I have stretch marks on the sides of my breasts, thighs, and lower stomach. I move to cover them with my hands. I find my wrists pinned to the bed on either side of my head as Myles kisses the ones he can reach on my chest.

He follows them with his tongue, making his own path when they end to my nipple which he gives a little nip to as if to reprimand me. Gasping each time his teeth glide over the sensitive peak, I arch deeper, back bowing towards him in offering. He does like to use teeth.

With a press to my wrists to make it understood my hands are to stay where they are, Myles lets go and moves down my body. His tongue laves into my belly button on his trek, teeth on my hip bones as he lifts first one leg over his forearm and then the other, opening me up for him.

His nose follows the natural path from my hip, down where the leg meets my core. Another deep breath before he dives in. I get no slow build up as his mouth suctions to my clit and I'm shouting to the rooftop at the feel of him eating like he is starving. I'm on the verge of orgasm when he pulls back, gliding his teeth over the swollen nub as he moves down. I hope he is going to do what he did on New Year's.

He does! That tongue dances around my entrance, spearing inside to move down and rim my asshole. I break position as I grab a handful of his hair at the back of his head, dig my heels into his back to hold him where he is, pulling at the sheets with my other hand, trying to keep myself from shooting off into space.

I earn a growl for that. And the vibration of it sends me into orbit. Tongue a hard appendage, he fucks me through my orgasm, lapping at all I give as I pulse and attempt to remember how to breathe. A sharp bite to my inner thigh has me gasping and clamping them on his head again.

Rearing up over me again, fists planted next to my head, I look up into those eyes that just slay me. Myles is exactly what I've been looking for. And for the moment, he is mine.

I lift a hand to cup his cheek as I shake off the thought that this doesn't mean anything more than what it is.

A kiss is pressed to my palm before that wicked mouth is on mine, sharing the taste of my pussy with me. Tongues dueling, I wrap my arms around him and a leg around his thick thigh and with a push with my other foot, I flip our positions. Thank you self defense classes because that was awesome.

Myles looks a little surprised to find himself on his back. I don't waste it in case he tries to take back the control he just lost and I make my move for that dick. Sucking the deep red head into my mouth, I get a taste of the precum that has been leaking out of him. Working to get him slicked up so he glides easy, I pump him in and out of my mouth, hand working in tandem.

Fingers sink into my hair as now it is Myles arching into the bed, heels planted on either side of my hips while I suck him as far down as I can. I move to cup and roll his balls, feeling them draw towards his body, cock pulsing against my tongue. He pulls me off him with a pop. "Stop. I'm not cumming in your mouth. I want to feel you clenching around my dick, not shooting down your throat."

I find myself on my back on the bed, our mouths fused again. The crinkle of a wrapper follows the sound of the bedside drawer. Myles kneels between my thighs, sheathing himself in latex and it is the hottest thing I've ever seen. With a pump to ensure the condom is on right, the man wraps a hand under my thigh and over my hip, jerking me up and to him.

Holding me slightly up so he can angle in, I can't help the small moan. "That is it baby, let me hear how you like it. Tell me I'm doing what you like."

My eyes pop open at the instruction. I'm used to holding back, but then we are the only ones here. No one to complain because they can hear what their neighbors are up to. No one to fear embarrassment if I'm too loud.

Myles bottoms out and I gasp loud and proud I took all of him. Hips undulate to meet each other, working at the common goal of getting each other off. I can feel the build up, the edge coming at me and before I can stop myself, I'm flying off with a cry that earns me another growl. Groins pressed together, Myles lets me ride the pulses as I pant as if I just ran a race.

Myles

Gritting my teeth, I count down from one hundred as Blanche milks at my cock. Her tight pussy is heaven and I want to stay there as long as possible. Her thighs are trembling and when I swipe a thumb over her swollen clit, she jolts like I shocked her.

Before she can so much as begin to protest, I have her flipped and on her knees. I press between her shoulders to have her chest as far down as she can go, presenting her pretty pussy, all puffy from my cock, for me. Her hands grabbed at the sheets as I notch back at her entrance. Surging in, shoving the air from her lungs in a gasp, I pull out, slow. I wait until she wiggles, making to move back on me, before repeating the move.

Memorizing the sounds she makes as I power into her, I begin speeding up as I feel my balls tighten. Hands tight on her hips, using them to pull her to me with more power. I pound her pussy. Her moans as she takes all I have to give are the most beautiful thing I've heard.

A hand leaves the sheets and comes back to land on my hip with a little push to signal she needs a moment. Grabbing it, I press it to the small of her back and slip my other hand around to the top of her slit, sliding down until I find the button that will make her go off like a rocket.

I can feel her pussy clamping down, ready to send her over once more. Not pausing my rhythm, I let go of the hand I have trapped and move to pull her up. Surging into her one final time, I sink my teeth into the place I call my spot. She screams as she comes around me and I regret the rubber barrier as I fill it instead of her.

Morning light wakes me and I reach for Blanche when I don't find her spooned up to me. Sitting up when I find the bed empty, I look around. She left.

Blanche

My car was freezing when I got into it before dawn ever broke the horizon. With a sniffle, I wrap the sleeves of the coveralls over my hands to help with the cold steering wheel as I make my way back to town.

This can't happen again. No more. Wiping the tears that keep sneaking out, I make the vow to myself that I'm done with men that don't want me. When I woke, I smiled at the way he held me pressed to his chest, his large back keeping me warm as all the bedding was still on the floor where I tossed it.

That smile quickly faded when I realized what I had done again. Falling into bed with a man that wanted something entirely different than I did. Dad has Dean and I know he will be fine as I make my way to my trailer. I left my phone at his house so I need to get back soon in case Dean needs me. I just need a moment or twenty.

I don't even attempt to stop the tears as I stand in my bathroom waiting for the water to heat at the thought of washing Myles off me. I can smell him in my hair, on my skin. With a little burst of anger at myself, I rip the curtain open and step into the spray that is still more cold than hot.

I'm pink from head to toe. I scrubbed and re-scrubbed myself to remove the night from me. He had me in every position

I could think of and some I didn't know were possible. I'm covered in beard burn that I couldn't wash off and there are several bruises from his liking of using his teeth. I can't argue I didn't like it as each time he sank those teeth into my skin, I came like a freight train.

Moving to my bed, I crawl beneath the blankets and stare at the window as it lightens.

CHAPTER ELEVEN

Christmas Not On Repeat

Blanche

Morning finds me still awake. Diving down into the memories of the last time I was with Myles was not the best way to spend the night. But it did do one thing for me.

I get out of the bed and begin texting Dad.

I need a tree and decorations, even the fake one he has stored in the spare room closet will do since there will be nowhere to get one on Christmas day. I grab a pen and my 'things to do' pad that has a cartoon mouse flipping the words off and start writing out a list for what I need for dinner. I did get Dean a couple gifts and had planned to give them to him this morning but I need to do this right. I need to make these memories with him.

If...

No, I stop that thought before it can formulate. I am giving my son his first Christmas. Me and Dad and Dean will celebrate. Let tomorrow sort itself out. My phone chirps and Dad is on his way with the tree so that we can have it up when Dean wakes. I love that man. No questions, just let him grab everything and a coffee and he was on his way.

Picking up scattered toys, I prepare the living room for the arrival of my son's first Christmas.

December Prior

Blanche

Opening my social media, I thumb through as I wait for my check up. The baby rolls and presses to my hand as I pet down my swollen stomach. After the 'people you may know' list I find the offered most recent posts.

Sitting up straight, I hover over the name of a group. Bryce Haine/Luske Lost And Found. Tapping it, I wait for it to load and then slam my hand over my mouth to stifle the full laugh that has several others in the waiting room looking at me for disturbing their peace.

Holy fucking shit. Bryce's face is plastered all over the group. It has his name listed as Haine hyphen Luske, but that is my husband. I send the group link to Dad. There is a short list of rules at the top and I read them over quickly.

One, don't comment if your name is not one of them mentioned.

Two, don't tag the mentioned person if they are already tagged.

Three, we know he is a piece of dog shit on a hot day that has turned white so we don't need to hear it here unless you are one of the mentioned.

Four, if you are one of the mentioned and don't want anything to do with this, message admin and you will be removed from all this drama.

Five, if you have the need for revenge, don't come to our town until you have calmed down. We love a good matinee but the same thing over and over gets old.

Five point subsection A, rethink revenge for a second time, he has a way of weaseling out of shit as his past shows.

This group is for educational purposes.

I snort again at the rules. There are twenty-three pictures of what looks like the poster you would put up if you lost a pet. Each one has a different woman's first name, quotes of what looks like texts of what Bryce told her to hook her in. No last names were used, but if anyone knows the woman and saw her with Bryce, putting two and two together won't be that hard. That has already happened since there are women tagged on some of the posts. The group has several thousand members in just the short time it has been live.

Comments are off the wall and some are kind of hilarious. Conversations between some of the women he has relationships with comparing things he does in bed and just the general Peter Pan syndrome has me laughing and not caring about the looks I'm being given. Some have tried to call it all lies but then receipts have been posted in the form of pictures and texts.

Dad messages me and I flip over to read it.

There is a lot of cursing and then the name and number of a lawyer that I am to call when I get done with my check up. He already contacted him and the ball is rolling. Bryce is in deep doo-doo.

Papers in hand, I find myself driving up the coast on a crisp winter day. Port Haven, Maine is around eleven hours but it will take me longer because I have to stop due to my pregnancy and I will be staying overnight half way. It was the only way Dad would let me make the trip myself. He wanted to close up the garage, but I couldn't let him do that with some jobs that have to be out before Christmas, and him down his two employees with the flu.

I creep into town well below the speed limit. It is so pretty. I would have loved to be here under different circumstances. Maybe Dad and I can return later. Main street is quaint with the little shops and I try to soak it all in. Small towns always have a hub and from the look of it, my choices are a hardware store or a coffee shop. Since I'm on the side of the street with the hardware, that is where I'll stop first.

The little porch and steps are clean of snow and ice, the bell jingles a welcome as I push open the wooden door that looks original to the building. It glides silent and effortlessly even though it must be nearly four inches thick. A man behind the counter is reading an instruction manual for the scanner he has laid out on the top that is stained nearly black with wear and age.

"Excuse me, I'm looking for Bryce Haine."

The most beautiful blue eyes look up from the papers in his hand. A quick sweep has them settling on my large belly leading the way. "You would be better off asking that question at Beanery."

Nodding, I take a mental picture of the man that embodies the term lumbersnack and turn to do as he said. Pregnancy hormones have me keeping a file of yummy men for my own clit flicks.

I'm glad that the sidewalks and street are ice free as I make my way across and into the warm glow of the most delicious smelling coffee shop. There are several people at tables scattered around the room but I'm drawn to the comfy looking couch with two women draped over it in what looks like boredom.

"Excuse me, I stopped across the road and the man sent me over here. I'm looking for Bryce Haine."

The only sound is the milk steamer as the room goes silent.

"Bryce? Can I ask why you are looking for him?" The little sprite of a woman behind the counter asks.

Digging in my bag, I take out the manila envelope I asked my lawyer if I could serve myself to the sorry excuse that I'm really not married to. "I need to give him these. That man said that you all could help me more than he could, so..."

The sound of a chair on the floor proceeds a talon-like hand that snaps into my field of view, "I'll take them."

Looking over at the woman standing next to me, I can't help finding her lacking. Sure the shell is pretty, but some of the most deadly things have the best disguises. I shove the packet back into my bag and cross my arms over my chest. "And why would I do that?"

Not a wrinkle or twitch comes to that heavily made up face as she narrows her eyes on me, "because he is my fiancé."

Cocking my head like I've seen Pepto do, I answer her, "well, I'm his wife."

If the silence earlier was loud, this one is an explosion. Two of the women look at me like I grew another head and it started speaking Shakespeare and the other one laughs before slapping her hand over her mouth. I like her, her cute little pin up like outfit with matching makeup suits her and makes me wish I wasn't so vanilla.

The nasty blonde next to me wrinkles her nose at the shorter of the two on the couch that laughed. I can't help bristling in preparation for defending her. "What is so funny?"

Not to be cowed by this woman who acts like she shits roses, the woman on the couch speaks up. "Girlfriend, fiancé, wife. Bryce has the trifecta."

A little mouse of a woman comes over, thumbs flying over her phone, "Veronica, maybe we should..."

I want to protect this one too as the ice queen shoots her a glare.

"Maybe you should listen to her Ronnie, you really don't need to be sweeping anything more under that rug. The lump is growing. And judging that bump there," the girlfriend points at where I'm rubbing my stomach, "it is only going to get bigger."

"Veronica." She actually enunciated her own name. "You are his *ex*-girlfriend. A gold digging whore that messed around with a man that is going to marry someone else. And this woman," she gestures in a dismissive way at me, "doesn't even have the right last name so there is no way in hell she is his wife. She is probably just as scheming as you, after the five seconds of fame that you all think you deserve from the future president of the United States. That kid isn't his either."

Ignoring Veronica, I hold my hand out to the ex-girlfriend to shake, "Blanche. Pleased to meet another gold digging whore."

Snickering, she shakes my hand over the back of the couch. "Chéri. Are you enjoying your five seconds of fame?"

Pressing my hand to my chest, I sigh as dramatically as I can, "I so am. Chasing a good for nothing fuckwad up the east coast is such fun. Sorry kid, your first word is so going to be fuck." I rub the little knot that is some appendage pressing from the inside in apology. Chéri introduces me to Winnie the Amazonian Queen and Keeley the Coffee Goddess.

The bell over the door gives a cheerful jingle and all eyes go to who entered. Ah, the fuckwad in question.

I don't know what I saw in him as Veronica tells him repeatedly that it isn't his kid. Dropping a truth bomb to all present that he is sterile. He didn't even pay attention to the papers I handed him he was so focused on my baby being his. I decide to drop a bomb of my own in this conversation to kill the thoughts of being a happy family I can see dancing in Bryce's eyes deader than a doornail. "Right, not Bryce's. The father's name is Christian. Christian Davies."

I did my research before coming here. I know who the blonde is and that she is the aunt to my unborn child.

"Well," you can hear the shock that Veronica is trying to hide under her ice queen facade, "now that we have established that that baby is not Bryce's, what do you want? Other than to claim that you are his wife."

Bryce winces and turns to Veronica. That look he uses to try to get out of trouble plastered on his stupid face. "She *is* my wife."

Veronica throws her hands up in the air. "For fuck's sake! She came in here looking for Bryce Haine. Haine! She doesn't even have the right last name to find you with."

Bryce looks at me with a brighter expression, maybe a little hope that I am here for him. Tracked him down because I love him and can't live without him. "Wait, how did you find me?"

"I'm glad you asked." I dig my phone out of my bag before tossing it to the couch. Tapping the screen, I pull up the page and flip it towards Bryce.

"A facebook group?" He scrolls down. With each post he pales a little more. Veronica is looking over his shoulder and shoves Bryce so hard his nose bounces off the screen.

Phones are being passed around again as everyone keeps up with the flow of conversation so much better than Bryce.

Customers are laughing now and reading comments out loud to their table partners.

I motion to the woman with the packet tucked under her arm, "you might want to take that to his lawyer. I just wanted the satisfaction of hand delivering it to him. Seems that blondie here is right, we aren't married."

Veronica starts to look smug.

"But there is a case of fraud in there. Seems marrying someone and giving a false name is just that. The state of Virginia sees it that way too."

The smug look disappears and her botox fails with the amount of anger she is displaying. "That is it. I've had it with you. If you hadn't used another name, you would be setting yourself up for bigamy charges if we had gotten married. Your stupidity just seems to be multiplying and I cannot do this anymore. We are done."

She steps out, slamming the door behind her before shoving it back open, "and you," she points at me, "you will be hearing from Christian's lawyers about..." she waves her hand, curling her lip at the bump under my kelly green sweater, "that."

"Are you sure it isn't my baby?" The man that came in with Bryce grabs him by the arm and drags him from the building followed by the woman who is now on the phone with who knows who. Poor clueless Bryce. If he wasn't such a waste of air, I'd be tempted to feel more sorry for him. But manwhores that think with their little heads for the majority of the time are not to be pitied.

Flopping on the couch, I realize I sat on my bag and yank it from behind me. "That was fun but now I'm more tired than driving up here made me."

Keeley comes around and starts laying out sandwiches and small bags of kettle cooked chips on the table in front of us. She sets a meal in front of me that has me drooling and the little man in residence doing flips. "So, what are you going to do now that you got even with the douche canoe?"

Deciding to stay over the week, the town is more than growing on me and think I want to stay. I got introduced to the whole group that comes with Winnie, Keeley, and Chéri. I'm sure that Chéri is dating two of the guys at the same time and no one cares. Just like in a real life, why choose romance story.

I got a show and dinner when we came across Bryce being left in the dust by Veronica. What really stuck with me was that Bryce got mad because she was sleeping with her bodyguards. Like he had any room to be offended. I hate double standards.

I'm now staying at Logan's inn and the view is just magnificent with the lighthouse and the winter waves. I've called Dad and filled him in on everything, including the feeling that I don't want to leave.

I'm headed to town to get myself something from Beanery when I find the road blocked. Police, EMS, and firefighters are all wrangling back a crowd that is trying to gawk at what is going on. Stepping out of my car onto the sidewalk, I crane to see what is going on. I can't tell, but it looks to be happening at the coffee shop.

I mumble under my breath and then nearly jump out of my skin as a voice answers from behind me.

Lumbersnack is standing close enough to have heard me over the crowd it seems and even though the breeze is quite brisk, I can smell his aftershave or something and he is so delicious. "When the shit hit the fan, Bryce went into hiding. He walked into Keeley's place from wherever he was holed up and they are now trying to get him out."

The crowd gives a cheer as Bryce is brought out in cuffs and placed in the back of a state trooper's car. I listen as people describe the things he has been up to, the most recent being attempting to attack Chéri after kicking in her apartment door. The details are being bandied about like the snowflakes the wind is swirling around us.

I rub my belly as the thought of dodging that bullet crosses my mind. I'm so glad that the baby I'm carrying isn't his if he is hiding those kinds of tendencies. Poor Chéri, she must have been terrified. The crowd is being shooed off. I give the man behind me a smile before darting around the police line and to the door that is being blocked by what appears to be sentinels with trooper badges.

"Excuse me, I need in there." Neither even look down at me and that is something that not many men can claim as I'm kind of tall for a woman. "Hello, pregnant lady, needing to pee."

Both sets of eyes flick down to me and then back to staring straight ahead, arms crossed over massive chests.

"I am not joking. I have a kid in here using my bladder as a trampoline and if you don't move, I am not above watering your shoes." I let the fear I just felt for Chéri tear up in my eyes as I give them a stern pout.

With a sigh, the one on the left shifts and lets me by. The jingle of the bells on the door has everyone present turning at my entrance. "Are you okay? I heard what he did at your apartment and I was scared shitless, then they wouldn't let us through while they did what they did. I was on my way in for a cookie. Now two giants are standing out there, keeping everyone out. I had to threaten to pee on their shoes to get them to let me inside. I might have even conjured some tears."

I trail off when I notice an older woman looking me over. She may be up there in years, but she doesn't look like a dummy.

"He did have good taste in women, like his grandfather. You know, I went to that group, looked up all those women. They were all over the map with looks and all were beautiful, some more unique than others, but still pretty. That Jordy was pretty damn funny with his little group and the pictures of those flyers."

I look at Chéri, who just shrugs. I'm then introduced and adopted by Bryce's grandmother. Seems I'm definitely not leaving town then.

CHAPTER TWELVE

Tiny Turkey & Of Course I Forgot Something

Blanche

The look on Dean's face when I carried him from the bedroom to see the tree all decorated and lit up was priceless. He sat in my lap on the couch clutching his lovie while the lights twinkled and Bing Crosby wished us a Merry Little Christmas.

He was more entertained by the boxes and paper and bows than the actual gifts we got him, but that is okay. He will play with it all later. Dad took so many pictures and little videos. Now to get dinner so we can do this day right.

I was surprised when I went online for the closest open grocery store to find the local one was open until four today. Good thing we are the only ones here besides the man who owns the place. Dean is in a mood with another tooth coming in. Fever, upset stomach with vomiting, diarrhea, constipation, in pain, cranky; every symptom to convince parents that their child has ebola but is just teething.

Dad is trying to help by walking with Dean instead of having him in the cart and has struck up a conversation with the man waiting to check us out. I check my list and head over to the canned goods aisle. I got all the fresh produce and one of the last turkeys, now for the rest of it and then I'm done.

Well, I guess we aren't the only ones here after all. Sheila stands in the middle of the lane looking at the cans of mushroom soup. I need those too for the green bean casserole but I'm not sure if I want to deal with her today. We can have normal green beans, I'll spruce them up with some bacon.

Glancing at my list, I roll my eyes at myself. I have to walk past her to get to the sweet potatoes. Time to act like an adult and just ignore her. It is Christmas, maybe she will pull the yule log out of her ass long enough to give it a break for one day.

I'm nearly past her when she turns and gives me her signature evil look. "Myles not invite you to the big party?"

I haven't seen Myles since Thanksgiving to be personally invited by him anywhere, not that that is any of her business. Grams made sure I got one having been in charge of the guest list. Not one of her little claimed family is going to be left out of a gathering. Dad was given an invite well before the final holidays set in when he was absorbed into Grams's group. Again, not that it is any of Sheila's business. "I was, but since this is Dean's first Christmas, Dad and I are having a smaller celebration."

Snarling her lip at the mention of Dean, Sheila tosses her hair off her shoulder. Strangely her tits aren't out for the world to see. But a mark on her shoulder catches my attention. The same shoulder the collar of her shirt is hanging off of. A perfect set of teeth marks with a purpling bruise on a specific spot on her shoulder. Resembling marks I myself have had on *my* shoulders. She smirks when she sees where I'm looking. "He likes to bite, doesn't he?"

I'm not even going to play dumb. My heart and brain are for once on the same page and both are screaming for me to retreat and lick my wounds. Myles can be with whoever he wants. He is a free agent. We have no commitments to each other. Those words ring true as I repeat them to myself. But why does my chest feel like it is caving in?

Sheila might be an awesome person to everyone but me and they could be happy. But something in me twists at the thought that he picked her over me. I'm mature in my answer. "Whatever."

She laughs at me as I push my cart by, heading for the end of the aisle. I need to get out of here before I snap and beat her head in with the can of soup she just picked up. The visions in my head have turned from me crying in the fetal position on the floor to violence with a thick coating of blood. "Did you really think he would pick you over me? Come on. Man like that needs someone who can take what he dishes out and come back for more. Not some frumpy little single mom. Ever wonder why he isn't with someone? Got kids? He isn't about that way of life. Likes being who he is. To come and go as he pleases. Doesn't want to be tied down with things like a family. Add in the fact that it is another man's kid, please. You need to wake the fuck up, honey."

Picking up my pace, I steer my cart down the pet aisle to get back to the front as soon as possible. Forget the rest of the list, we will make due.

"You think that since he fucked you in his greenhouse that he wants you? You're not the first and will not be the last. I've been there plenty of times. Add in the tree farm, his house, the hardware, his truck. You name it, I've been there with him. And so have plenty of other women. You are just a novelty. Once the shine wore off your penny, he was right back with me."

Sheila follows me as I make my way to the front, only stopping her hissing tirade when Dad comes into view. I hold my tears back as I place the things I already had in the cart on the belt system and move to the keypad to swipe my card and pay.

Dad keeps looking between me and the woman standing behind me. Sheila offers him a sweet smile as she places the item divider on the belt and her hand basket behind it like she didn't just tear out my heart. "Hello Mister Deveraux, hope you are having a nice Christmas with your grandson. First memories are precious. You only get to make them once."

Is she fucking kidding me? I spin to tell her where she can go when I spot Richard. He has his phone out, appearing like he is scrolling but the angle is wrong and his thumb isn't moving. He's recording this interaction. I turn back around before Dad can notice him.

"Forty-three oh eight."

Nodding, I slide my card, push the pin in and grab the handles of the bags before the slip is even printed. "Merry Christmas."

"Happy Hanukkah. I'm Jewish dear, reason I'm here today. That and there is always someone who needs just one more thing. I like to think of myself as helping them have the best memories if I'm here for them when they need something." The little tag on his shirt reads Aaron.

"I almost named my son Aaron." Dean is looking at the little man in the apron behind the counter.

Aaron offers him a cookie from the box next to the register. "And what fine name did he end up with instead?"

"Dean." I smile as my son offers Aaron a bite of his cookie. Aaron takes a cookie out and taps it against Dean's before popping it into his mouth. Sheila has her arms crossed over her huge tits, foot tapping on the floor as she waits her turn to check out.

Dean smiles at Aaron and takes a big bite to copy him. "That is a strong name for a strong little boy. What made you pick that over the awesome name that is Aaron?"

My smile falls. "I named him after a friend that was there when he was born." With that, we leave the store.

"Miss Deveraux."

I turn from buckling in Dean to find Richard coming towards me. "I really don't have the time today to deal with you."

He nods and shows me that his phone is not recording. "I just want to say that my being here has nothing to do with you. Well, it does since I was hired to follow you. I'm sorry for that. And I'm sorry that all this is happening. But I want to let you know that nothing I have turned in is in any way incriminating or shows you in a bad light. You're a good mom. Merry Christmas."

Folding my lips into my mouth, I nod and get into the car with Dad and Dean. I'm fighting the tears that wanted to start when Sheila opened her mouth and more now that he said what he did.

Dean is on the living room floor playing with his new toys and Dad is in the kitchen starting dinner. It is a little after ten in the morning and I have had a hell of a day. I need five minutes.

The bathroom off my room is the farthest from the living area and that is where I go. Turning the faucet on the sink to full blast, I sink down the wall and bury my face in my knees and just let the tears flow.

Sniffling, I reach above my head for the box of tissues to find it empty. Opening the cabinet next to me, I look for the extra box and see something else that gives me pause. There, set between my tampons and the wall, a blue and pink box. A box that I bought as part of a two pack when I needed to see if I was sure when I thought I was pregnant with Dean.

Abandoning the tissues, I pick up the box of tampons and the pregnancy test in each hand, focusing on my mental calendar.

Oh fuck.

Dropping the boxes, I snag my phone from the floor next to me and pull up my period app. I had turned off the notifications after Dean's birth because I was a little irregular to start and it was annoying, chirping at me several times a day. When it finally became regular, I'd not turned it back on. And now I missed something I needed to know in a bad way. I was late, by two months. Almost three.

I flipped through my contacts and selected the one person I knew would talk some sense into me. I didn't even wait for a greeting when the ringing stopped. "Grams. Go somewhere private."

I could hear people asking where she was going but she ignored them, not replying as I heard the sounds of them fading. The latch of a door had complete silence from the other end. "I got a hunch what you are about to tell me, but I'll let you say it instead of guessing."

Deep breath, "I'm pretty sure I'm pregnant."

"Uh-huh. And is it who's I think it is?"

This is what I needed. No girly squealing like one of the others would have been doing, drawing attention to this conversation. "Yes."

"And what are you going to do about it?" I can hear her tapping her nails on something.

"Can we switch to a video call?" I need to see her face and I don't know why. I really need her here, but I know she is at

Myles's house and that would raise a whole lot of flags that the nosey noses we call a family would want to inspect.

There is a beep and I can see Grams in her elf hat and ears as she sits in what looks like the bathtub in the downstairs lavatory. Why she is in the tub and not sitting on the toilet, or even the counter, is not a question I need answered. "Better?"

I nod and sniffle, pulling the box of tissues out that resulted in this epiphany. "So we were at the grocery store, and I ran into Sheila."

Grams nods as she opens a bottle of shampoo and sniffs it before putting it back on the ledge at the back of the tub, "of course you did. And what did the skank have to say?"

I love this woman for not bringing me back to the reason I called her and letting me work through more than my current issue. Reaching up, I turn off the sink because now all it is doing is make me want to go pee. "She was sporting a mark. The same kind I've been seen wearing a couple times the last year."

Grams turns the bottle of body wash that is obviously Myles's that she was sniffing up and starts squeezing it out. Petty, but right now I like it. "Oh, really."

"Really. I've had my suspicion he was seeing her after all the times she went into the store so much this summer, but she just confirmed it. She told me that Myles wasn't interested in a relationship or kids, especially ones with the drama I have attached. I'm paraphrasing of course."

Bottle empty or nearly so, Grams fills it back with water and puts it on the shelf. "Is he now? Here I thought the boy had more sense than to mess around with that woman. You would think he would have learned his lesson about that family when he dated Carla. Sheila acted like he was hers and not her sister's. Hell, Todd acted the same way just with the store, going in and taking whatever he wanted for his handyman business. It got to be too all much and Myles called it off with Carla. Helen and I had to do some damage control when they started spreading rumors. When we sent Todd a bill for what he took from the store with a letter we had Dylan draft up was when they left him alone. Well, as alone as a desperate woman can be. Guess Sheila finally wore him down."

With a sniffle, I toss the nasty tissues into the trash that are littered around my butt. "Richard was in the store too. Pretty sure he got the whole thing on camera."

Grams curses and begins dumping shampoo out next.

"He stopped me in the parking lot and told me that he sees nothing wrong in the evidence he has turned in, and that he is sorry for the job he's been hired to do, that I'm a good mom."

Grams stuffs some toilet paper in this one, adds water and gives it a shake before returning it to the shelf. "That brought on the tear fest?"

I watch as she wiggles out of the deep tub that has her nearly folded in two with the tall sides of it. I loved that tub the first time I saw it. Big, clawfoot cast iron, deep. Perfect for a bubble bath. "And needing tissues found the test that had me calculating and realizing that I'm more than likely pregnant."

Grams snorts at the 'more than likely'. "So pee on it."

"Um, you're on the phone."

Setting her phone on the counter, I watch as she opens drawers before smiling when she finds toothpaste and some kind of cream. She squeezes the toothpaste into the sink and then begins refilling it with what I can now see is muscle rub. I make a mental note in huge neon to never make her mad with access to my stuff. "So? We're both human, have the same bodily functions, pee."

Flipping the box over, I reread the instructions when I see the embossed date. "It is expired."

"Well go get a new one. I'm texting Aaron now to make sure he has what you need." I can see her thumbs moving where the keyboard would be.

"Aaron? I just met him today, do you know everyone?"

All the answer I get is a duh face while she resumes squeezing more cream into the toothpaste tube.

I shove everything back under my bathroom cabinet and head to the living room. Dean is napping on the floor where he played himself to sleep and Dad is still in the kitchen. "I'll be back, I forgot some things and it just isn't Christmas dinner without sweet potatoes."

Dad doesn't look up from where he is assembling his cranberry salad when he answers, "get some cream of mushroom soup too."

CHAPTER THIRTEEN

Babysitters, Grocery Stores, Hunky Men

Blanche

Aaron meets me at the door to the store and hands me a cardboard box before steering me to the bathroom. "I'll set the timer when you tell me to."

Grams's voice from my phone has me squawking. I didn't even remember to hang up. "Told you Aaron would help."

Looking at the screen that is laying on the giant toilet paper dispenser, I see Grams has wandered into what looks like Myles's office. "Don't touch anything in there."

I don't know why I'm whispering. "Too late."

Rolling my eyes at the laugh that comes from the space in the bathroom near the counter, I shove my dignity down with my pants and pee on the stick. "Time."

Three minutes and twelve seconds later there are for sure two pink lines. I've had two panic attacks. And one king size dark chocolate candy bar. I'm sitting on the stool behind the belt for the cash register with Grams on the phone in front of me and Aaron sitting on the conveyor. "Now what?"

I look at Aaron and shrug. "What if what Sheila said was true?"

Grams scoffs from where she is stringing all the paperclips she can find, including three new boxes, together. "That woman has been chasing him since high school. She stopped speaking to her own sister and chose to spread her own family gossip that should have remained private when he picked Carla over her. The shit she had been saying about you is the same game she always plays and people have learned to ignore her. That is why the town still loves you and hates her."

Aaron looks at me and then at the camera, shaking his head, "so why are you doing that?"

I told him about the bathroom pranks when I was stuffing my face with chocolate and all he did was laugh. "Because if that man did finally give in, when he had a perfectly good woman waiting on him to pull his head out of his ass, he deserves the things I can think up. And he deserves this and more for being so stubborn when it comes to manning up. I might even turn Jordy loose on him. Or kick him in the dick."

Aaron and I share concerned faces. Picking at a snag in my leggings, I voice my biggest fear, "what if I'm too much? What if the drama that comes with me is too much? What if the fact he will have to spend the rest of his life with another man's son is too much? What if they take Dean and the resulting fall out is too much? What if I am too vanilla? What if…"

"What if you are secretly an alien and instead of you probing us, we are sending Myles to probe you and all you want to do is gather acorns and go home?" Grams stops my rant mid sentence and Aaron nearly falls off the belt laughing at her. "Point me to the person that filled your head with all that and I will kick their ass."

I can feel the blush heating my cheeks as I rip open a second candy bar and stuff half in my mouth.

"I thought so. You listen and you listen well. No person is too much for anyone. If someone ever tells you that you are too much, you walk your happy ass out that door and don't look back. You can't help if they aren't enough to handle all of

132

you. And you need someone that is capable of handling all of you. You don't make yourself into something or someone you aren't just to make it work for them. I've half a mind to tell Lance the shit that just came out of your mouth. He'd be very disappointed knowing you think that of yourself.

"Now wipe your nose, fix your hair because it looks as if you have a rat's nest on the top of your head, pull up your big girl panties, and decide on the future you want. If you want Myles, go for it. If you want to move on, do it. I know you are stronger than you are currently feeling. Look what you did when you set out on the path to confront Bryce. Look what you have. And don't you dare bring up that ridiculous custody shit. They don't have a leg to stand on and they know it. Dean needs you to set your crown on straight and be the hero in his story. And if Myles is too stupid to see the powerhouse you are, that the two of you could be together, then he isn't the man for you."

Aaron starts a slow clap that echoes around the empty store.

My phone chirps with an incoming message. I can't help the huge gasp that comes out of me at the image that loads from the text Dad just sent. There is a fire extinguisher dripping foam on my floor next to what was once our turkey. "I need to go home. Dad tried burning down the kitchen. This is why he doesn't cook anything other than instant meals or stuff not requiring a stove."

Aaron leans to look at the screen and laughs. "It is too late to get a new one cooked in time or I'd send one with you."

Grams sits up and looks around at her handy work. "You can't go home yet, you haven't made a decision on what to do. If you go home, you will just ignore it and now you have no turkey."

This time the look Aaron and I share is full of suspicion. His phone chirps, his eyes going big at whatever he just got.

"She's right. You need to think and your dad, other than trying to burn down the house, can handle things a little longer. Maybe we should go look at those dinner trays, I think I got a turkey one. Better than nothing."

Now I know she is up to something and Aaron just got wrangled into it. But I do need something for dinner and those trays aren't bad if you add some spices. "Fine, let's go look and I need some sweet potatoes and mushroom soup."

Myles

Grams disappeared about an hour ago and then sent me a text from who knows where that we needed cranberries. Real ones. So she could use them as garnish in the drinks. With a sigh, I head out to my truck in the snow. It sure is pretty but the beauty is lost on me with Blanche staying at home this year.

She gave some lame excuse about it being Dean's first and wanting it to be spent as just her and her dad but we all know it is the impending hearing about custody. I know that it is illegal, but I broke into Dylan's office and read her file. How else am I to protect her if I'm missing key details?

They threatened her. They threatened Dean.

I cornered that PI that has been slinking around the day he first served her with papers and the man is actually half decent. He told me that he is doing all he can to help her. He doesn't mind the sleazy job he does, but when it is to find dirt on good people, he tries his hardest not to.

I should have taken Dylan's fancy ass car. It has heated seats and I will be nearly in town before my truck even thinks about blowing anything but freezer cold air at me. The lot at Port Grocers is nearly empty. Aaron's car and another I don't recognize immediately are the only ones there.

Hand on the keys dangling from the dash, I debate leaving the beast running so it will be warm when I get back in. No one is around and if there was, only Dylan would mess with it, so I leave it running.

The store feels hollow without anyone shopping. On any given day, there is always a cashier and at least three people picking something up they need. The produce is back near the meat counter. I cut down the household aisle, pausing at the baby stuff, before moving on to get what her ladyship asked for.

Cranberries in hand, I turn to see Aaron disappear down the canned goods section. I need him to check me out, so I follow.

Stopping in my tracks, I see the person I was just thinking about standing there debating between name brand and generic soups. She has a frozen meal of some sort under her left arm and a can of sweet potatoes in the crook of her elbow. Leggings, her dad's sweater, boots tied around themselves so she can slip them off when needed. Her toboggan has a large poof ball on the top that moves when she does. "Aaron, what is the difference between these?"

She looks towards the front of the store for the man in question before turning to where I'm standing. She gives a start and then narrows her eyes at me.

I've got a mom, a sister, multiple cousins, and several female friends so I know that look. That look says I'm in trouble. Not that I know what I did. Might as well jump before she tells me how high and try to figure it out with how to fix it. "Price, sometimes quality. I can vouch for the cheaper one, tastes better to me."

Grabbing the can off the shelf, Blanche stomps off towards the front. Yeah, I'm in trouble. Glutton for punishment that I am, I just ask. "What did I do?"

Aaron rolls his eyes at me and starts ringing up Blanche's purchases.

"How's Sheila?"

That was out of left field. "I wouldn't know."

Blanche nearly flings her card at Aaron when she pulls it from the pocket on the back of her phone. "No? I guess she is just what you are looking for then. Don't have to keep tabs on her, just fuck her where and when you want, then move on. Seems to be your MO."

I step back at the venom in her voice and the word fuck leaving her lips. "What are you talking about? If you're saying I'm seeing Sheila, then you got rocks for brains woman. I wouldn't touch that with Bryce's dick. In fact, he never even touched her if that tells you anything."

Aaron's watching us like we are the most interesting thing to happen to him all day. The man could speak up, even to back me up on how liberal Sheila is with her favors. But no, he just keeps silent. I'll remember that, buddy, next time one of the coolers needs to be fixed.

Blanche tosses her head and that damn ball on top almost makes me laugh but I bite it back. That would be a death sentence to laugh at her right now. "So a woman who gets around is... is..."

"Double standards. Men can but women can't." Thank you Aaron, thank you. He holds up his hands and hops up on his stool at my glare.

"Right. I hate that shit. Not saying that she doesn't deserve the hate she gets for the other shit she does, but that is just wrong. Especially if you are sampling the goods yourself." Blanche grabs the bag of food and makes to leave before spinning back at me, "she has a bite."

Now we are cooking with gas. I know exactly what has been going on. I saw Sheila a couple days ago and she was showing off a gnarly mark on her shoulder. "And she said I did it?"

Blanche looks ready to cry. Now that I'm looking at her without her mad on, I can see she has been doing just that. Then it hits me, how is she here and I don't know it. Her phone is in her hand. I'll have to check on that once I get this sorted. "She said that you wouldn't want a vanilla flavored baby daddy drama llama."

Llama? She called Blanche a llama? Why a llama? I don't have time to figure that one out. Pulling her into my arms, I suck in a breath of the smell of her honey vanilla shampoo that clings to the cap she wears. "Sweets, my favorite flavor is vanilla. I take a bite out of it any chance I get. And the baby daddy drama isn't going to chase me off. I've been wracking my brain for ways to help you. When they threatened the two of you, it was all I could do to keep from going down there and taking care of them myself."

Sniffles are the only answer I get.

"Blanche, Sweets, come on. She was lying. I don't know who bit her, but it wasn't me. And whatever else she said, even calling you a llama, it was all lies. Something she is good at."

Aaron taps Blanche on the shoulder and hands her a tissue. "See, we told you."

We? Who else has she been talking to? Aaron holds up his hands again and backs back to his stool.

"Do you even want to be a daddy?"

CHAPTER FOURTEEN

Lonely Hearts & Cranberries

Blanche

Before I tell him he has a kid on the way, I need to know how he feels. I won't trap a man with a child. That never works out for anyone, especially the kid. I don't know what I will do if he says he doesn't want kids, move again maybe.

Myles's big chest fills with air when he sucks in a deep breath. "More than anything. I've wanted them for a long time, just never found the woman that called to me on a deep enough level to make that family with. Because it is a package deal. Wife and kids."

I know what he just said, but I need a detail ironed out. "When Dean called you Dada, you didn't look happy about it."

Heaving another sigh, Myles puts his forehead on top of my head. I love that he is so tall, makes me feel normal, "I was over the moon. And then it hit me that I wasn't his daddy. That you might not want me to be. That I might not measure up."

Huh. Seems like the 'I'm not good enough' train has more than one passenger.

I know I look like hell, but I need to see his face. "Really?"

Myles dips down and gives me a gentle kiss. "Really. You want to know a little secret?"

I can see Aaron nodding along with me out of the corner of my eye, his hands clasped in front of his chest, an adorable look on his face thanks to our sappiness.

"Since the moment you walked into my store, I've wanted you. And then you stayed and I got to know you and I wanted you even more. The fact you were pregnant never bothered me. The fact that it could have been Bryce's, didn't bother me. Dean isn't mine? Says who? I was there when he took his first breath and I want to be there for more firsts. I want to make memories with the both of you."

And that is why I'm pregnant. This man makes my ovaries explode. "And if I was to tell you that there will be two babies by next Christmas for you to love?"

Myles doesn't even take a moment to process. Sweeping me into his arms, face buried in my hair. His breath trembles as he exhales before pressing his lips to my forehead. "Are you sure?"

"Test didn't even hit five minutes and those lines were bright pink." I had forgotten we weren't alone. Aaron was a witness to that test popping positive faster than the done timer on a turkey.

Setting me back on my feet, Myles cups my face in his big, work roughened hands and kisses me stupid. Not a thought in my head when he is done. I'm pretty sure that I wouldn't be standing if it wasn't for his hands on me. "Come home with me. We'll stop and get Lance and Dean. Aaron, you're coming too. Shut the doors and meet us there."

"I thought you had to pick the cranberries yourself."

Grams greets us like there are not extra people coming in the door behind Myles. Myles turns to take Dean from me, seeing to his winter wear, allowing me to take off my own coat and boots first for the first time in a long time. The food we made is being integrated into the buffet laid out on the counters and everyone welcomed us like we were just late and had not been planning to skip.

Myles hands the bag of berries to Grams who tosses them behind her into the container that has all the ice before opening her arms to Aaron. "Sweetie, so glad you could get here in time for dinner."

"Wouldn't miss it for anything." Aaron embraces her, before working his way through the crowd with greetings of cheer.

"How was it that I just happened to show up to the grocer at the same time as Blanche?" Myles cuddles Dean, handing him a teether from the fridge he is bumping closed with his hip.

He has supplies here for my son. Our son, if his little admission in the store is anything to go by. I might need to be a little more cynical, my track record with men in the last few years speaks for itself. Because this time, it feels different. So different. And I want it to matter. To stick.

"Christmas magic." Grams flutters her hand at him over her shoulder before turning to making some kind of mixer she garnishes with the cranberries and a cinnamon stick. "No alcohol," she says as she hands it to me.

I'm not sure what they are talking about, it seems like code for something. I'll ask later.

"Sure, we will call it that." Myles grabs my free hand with his and tugs us into the living room. I'm given his recliner that molds around me like butter and is oh so comfy as he sits on the floor.

Dean is now in the center of the room, right next to the soaring pine that twinkles with lights and covered in just the right amount of decorations, topped with a beautiful star. His eyes are huge as he gums the jelly cold ring in his little fist. Reaching for one of the remaining boxes underneath, Myles sets it in front of Dean and picks at it to get his attention.

The room is in one of those silences that is peaceful. Everyone watching a little boy open his gifts and the magic of his wonder at the occasion is beautiful. Each strip of paper is pulled and handed to Myles as a box is revealed with no outer markings. Logan helps fold the flaps down and Dean leans over to look in with an exclamation. His little hand darts in and comes up with a little wooden hammer. As he turns and almost smacks Myles in the face to soft laughter from all of us, Logan lifts out a small tool carrier. Obviously hand made by the man holding my son. Dean plops down next to it and begins pulling everything out, chattering and showing each piece to Myles.

Dad sits down on the arm of the chair I'm in and pulls me into his side. Myles has to keep distracting Dean from the tools to open the other gifts. Every household here got him something it would seem.

"My turn." Grams motions to Rhiannon and the two of them disappear from the room, returning with a wrapped gift that is obviously an large animal.

Dean is awestruck sitting back in Myles's lap, little mouth hanging open. With a little coaxing, he is up and helping Grams pull the paper off. It is one of those rideable horses for toddlers in brown with a black mane and tail. "And when you get older, I'm gonna make Logan move that piece of shit float out of my stables and you are getting a real one. Then you and I will go riding down the beach like I used to."

"You are going to make him say things that will get him kicked out of daycare." Myles is placing the tools back into their box as he chastises Grams. "Not that I really want him going back there. Melody is great at what she does, but Carla... Plenty of people to keep him entertained in his own home."

The room pauses and all eyes are on me. Myles looks up from stuffing paper into the biggest box to see everyone looking at us and realizes what he said.

Dylan pulls what looks like a twenty from his wallet and hands it to Grams. Dad blusters, pointing a finger at the two of them, "don't give her that, she cheated."

Grams stands with her hands on her hips and glares across the room at him. "I did not. You were trying to cheat when you set that turkey on fire."

"Dad! You set fire to my turkey on purpose? I wondered how a nearly raw bird bursts into flames." I shove at him to get him off my chair.

Hands in the air like I'm some wild animal about to jump him, he backs away. "Now Princess, it was for a good cause. You two needed a little nudge. Mix a little of this and a little of that and you have a controlled burn. You had a fire extinguisher, so there was no harm. Except for that poor bird. Grant was on the phone the whole time."

Grant lets off an grunt when Chéri elbows him with a glare.

Dylan hasn't released the bill in his hand and Grams is trying to pry it from him without ripping it. "How did she cheat?"

Grams shoots Dad another dirty look, but that doesn't stop him since she threw him under the bus in return. "She texted me to do something to get you and Dean to the party. When I told her you had to run back out for things you forgot, she said she had a plan and would send Myles out to talk some sense into you. That you had something to tell him anyways. She never called off the drastic measures. What did you have to tell him? I don't remember you saying anything about needing to talk to him."

"I never told you to burn the kitchen down." Grams has given up on getting the twenty from Dylan now that it is obvious my dad was a stool pigeon.

My turn to glare and it is aimed at the old woman who is now trying to look casual in the rocker set near the tree. "That is between me and Myles."

Grams waves her hand regally before picking up Dean who is wanting in her lap. "You might as well tell them. You won't be hiding it much longer."

"I wasn't hiding it, I only figured it out today." I don't know how I'm talking as I have my teeth clenched so hard my jaw aches.

Everyone is looking around at everyone else. Myles is trying to hide a smile as he cleans up the Christmas Wrapping strewn about. Grams is mouthing one side of Dean's teether as he giggles at her. I can't help the defeated sigh that leaves me at the reiteration there will be no secrets from this crew. I catch Myles's eye and he winks at me. Just as I'm about to tell them, Dylan figures it out.

"Greenhouse!"

I'm going to kill him. Now I know why Myles tried so many times when they were kids. The others don't need to know the details, even if he is wrong.

"Oh. OHHHHHH!" Chéri is pointing between Myles and I with big eyes.

Keeley has her eyes squinted at us, looking like something isn't adding up. "No, that can't be it. She would be much bigger."

"Does everyone know about the damn greenhouse?"

Myles makes a lunge for Dylan who darts around the couch, scooping Dean from Grams and holding him in front of him like a shield, "let's go see what we can find you to eat? Bet you're hungry."

"Dylan." Myles growls at his brother as everyone follows back to the kitchen and dining room. Grabbing my hand, he tucks me up under his arm and kisses the top of my head. "Sorry, Sweets. He has a big mouth. What makes him a good lawyer is he has his nose in everything."

In the dining room, I find Winnie pulling a high chair to the table. This isn't the same one from Grams's house. This one, like the crib, is wooden. It shows true craftsmanship instead of the cheap stuff you get in a store. I tear up a little at even more signs that the man at my side wants what I have to offer.

"This was our chair, many a Carver has sat here and many more too thanks to your new daddy. Same as that crib." Dean stops wiggling to listen to what Dylan is saying while buckling him, Winnie adjusts the tray and Logan waits with a plate of food. I can see that it is mashed and little bits, just how he needs it. Tony stands with a sippy cup, waiting for his turn to serve the little prince. These people should never be left out of moments that make memories. I was wrong and can see it.

Myles tilts up my chin with his finger and kisses me. The room erupts in applause and cheers. Dean is clapping a mashed potato sprinkler on anyone near.

"Want to tell them?" he whispers on my lips.

Nodding, I cling to him, burying my face in his chest.

"She's pregnant, we're gonna have another baby." The room is even louder if possible.

145

I sniffle, getting a small hug in before I'm swept from Myles. Many a teary eye and not just the women. Myles is being congratulated as much as I am. Looking over Chéri's shoulder, he meets my gaze as Dylan hugs him. I love that he said we. I can't hold back another admission. I mouth the words to him. I love you.

Myles reaches for me as his brother lets go, sweeping me into his arms. Face nuzzling mine, "I love you, Sweets."

CHAPTER FIFTEEN

Christmas Magic & Happy Endings

Myles

I watch my family as they celebrate the final holiday of the year.

My family.

I love that.

I don't mean Dylan or the other people that moved into my life and never left. I mean the woman beside me and the little boy between us. The life she grows.

The front door slams open and I start from my chair, as do several of the other guys.

"You cheating hussy!"

"Mom?" Dylan and I say together. I don't know who is more surprised; us, who took her to the airport just yesterday or Grams, who chokes on what she is calling holiday happy juice.

"The plan was that if they didn't figure it out themselves by New Year's Eve that we would step in. Then, not now. You cheated." Mom is wagging her finger at Grams as she stomps through the house followed by Pops and Marley.

Pops stops next to me and gives me a one armed hug. His other sleeve hangs empty at his side. Mom must have been in such a hurry that she didn't let him put his prosthetic back on after the flights. Getting it through security is a bitch if they keep making him take it off and he loves the looks on their faces when they x-ray his carry on and see an arm. "Heard you got some news to share."

Marley grabs the hunk of breast meat off Dylan's plate when he gives her a hug, dancing away when he goes after it. I glare at him as he gives up and sits back down. "Someone has a big mouth."

Mom turns from her stare off with Grams, "it wasn't your brother, this time. Your dad's new bestie spilled the beans last night. Something about a big plan to get you two together today."

I look at Blanche, who is just as confused as me. The big news? We *just* announced...

Grams gasps in mock affront. "Lance, how could you? This was supposed to be a top secret mission. I'm not splitting the pot with you now."

Mom spins back to Grams, "you didn't win. You cheated. I think everyone should get refunds."

Marley grabs a glass of wine and takes a deep drink to clear her chipmunk cheeks of turkey before speaking, "I think Myles and Blanche should get the money. Like a baby gift."

And there it is. No secrets.

"Baby?" Mom and Pops both shout as they round on me. The house seems to have an echo. "Why didn't you tell us?"

I glare at Dylan who takes his phone off the table and shoves it in his pants pocket, Blanche nods and is swept into a hug from my mom.

"I'm getting two grandbabies for Christmas? Oh, I wonder what they should call me?" Mom now has Dean out of his chair and is snuggling him, kissing his food-caked cheeks.

"I thought the big announcement was the two of you finally got your shit together, before that little guy graduated high school at the rate you were going." Pops smacks Dylan in the back of the head on his way past, "stop fighting with your sister." He clasps my shoulder and I can tell by the grin on his face, he is about to give me shit. "Not that I'm complaining cause I got two new kids to spoil, but I gave you boys the talk. Raincoats."

Dylan chokes on the turkey he just stole back from Marley. She slams him on the back with enough force it launches from his mouth and plunks onto Keeley's plate.

"You nasty man." Keeley snarls her lip in disgust at the masticated food on her plate.

Dylan still can't talk so he makes motions like it wasn't his fault and points at Marley to blame her.

Blanche has come to a pause and is looking at me curiously. Her eyes unfocused and I can see the wheels turning. Fuck, I should have told her when I knew, but I secretly hoped. Wanted to lock her to me any way possible. Looking around, the others are wondering now too, thanks to Pops. We are all adults and everyone will know eventually, so might as well spill it in front of them. "It broke."

"I'm a sperm magnet. Or a condom jinx. A baby factory. I'm gonna end up barefoot and pregnant for the rest of my life." She looks down at her stomach, "what is wrong with you? One baby daddy isn't enough? Want to go for a trifecta? Three's a crowd but others say the third time's the charm."

I gather her up as she collapses in her chair in tears. Lance hands me a handkerchief, a real one. One of those big paisley ones. "Better keep those handy, she was a water fountain the last go round too. Cried over a dog food commercial."

"I did not." Blanche shoves at my chest to shoot her dad a look. "It was a music video."

Winnie nods from where she has been sitting with Logan, Grant, Tony, Aaron, and Chéri watching the drama unfold. Dinner and show is a theme around here it seems. "I bet I know the one, by Lewis Capaldi?"

Blanche nods and blows her nose in the cloth with a sly look up at me, before handing it back to her dad. He doesn't even bat an eye, just shoves it back into his pocket.

Marley notices Aaron and lets out a squeal. "Carter!"

"Bobbie!"

Blanche looks at me, confusion written on her face as I let her go to sit back down. "She and Aaron and a guy named Brandon were friends in school. She calls him Carter for Aaron Carter and he calls her Bobbie for Bob Marley."

Pops has pulled up another chair and is digging into the loaded plate Mom set in front of him. "All my kids have famous names. I taught music for a time after..." He waves what is left of his arm, making the sleeve flap. "Myles Davis, Bob Dylan, Bob Marley."

I see her look at the empty fabric and whisper in her ear. "A tree was down and he tried working it himself. I'll tell you more later. It don't slow him down and he hates being babied. Mom making his plate shows how tired he is. And don't worry about Dean, he helped raise us and tons of cousins."

She nods before scooping Dean back from where he made the round of the table once again. He was with Marley, who is sitting next to her, trying to eat with one hand but not having the practice of doing so with a baby in her lap.

"Hello?"

Blanche

The men in the room go on alert again. Somehow we missed the open front door. Probably due to the overheated room and all the excitement.

The man standing on the rug just inside the door is so out of place. Most of us are wearing holiday pajamas or lounge clothes. Myles's parents and sister are the only ones in normal clothes as even Myles is wearing flannel pants and a tee. The interloper is in a three piece suit that costs more than my car.

I would still recognize him anywhere though.

Christian Davies.

The man standing behind him on the porch in the blue trench coat isn't a welcome sight at our gatherings either, even if he said something nice to me the last time we ran into each other. Was that only this morning?

"Christian?" I hug Dean closer to me as Christian takes me saying his name as an invitation to come on in. Richard is a smart man and stays on the outside.

"I came to talk. Can we go somewhere?" He looks around the full table and the many hostile faces. Chéri is filling in Aaron and Logan is doing the same to Marley, neither using library voices so it is obvious who they are talking about.

Winnie reaches for Dean and takes him from the room followed by Keeley. Dylan places himself between where they just went and Christian.

I'm tired of cowering in fear from this family. My strength is in this room. Time I use it. "I don't think so. You can say anything you have to in front of everybody. I'll just tell them later and this will save me having to repeat whatever you say."

Christian nods as he looks around again. He is a Senator and lawyer, so used to being in front of a crowd, speaking his side of things. We will see if what he says will be anything we want to hear. "I've got something for you."

He snaps his fingers and Richard comes in with another manila packet before retreating back to where he is leaning up against the porch railing.

Dylan snatches it from Christian as he holds it out to me. "As Miss Deveraux's legal counsel, I'll take that and look over it for her."

When I make no move to correct Dylan, Christian nods and turns back to me. "My sister overstepped. She can get...overzealous, in her attempts to help me further my career. The papers you signed after you told me about the baby still hold. Those," he motions to the handful Dylan is reading, "will reinforce them. Keeping what happened from happening again. It was never my plan to take Dean from you. I don't want children. Never did, never will. In fact, I got a vasectomy after you got pregnant."

I look to Myles, who reaches over and takes my hand, giving it a reassuring squeeze.

"No one will come for your son again. Not my sister, not my family. No one. He is yours. Forever and always." Christian turns, leaving behind him a shocked silence. He stops in the door, looking over his shoulder at me and then Myles. "There was something that turned up in the investigation that Mister Yokum conducted. He reported it to me and only me. I see no reason for it to become public knowledge or my family to know."

He is baiting me and I can't resist. "What? I thought Richard said I was a good mom."

Christian looks at the man on the porch and back at me, "Richard?"

I can't help the blush that turns me a shade close to the red of the tablecloth. "Private investigator, detective, dick. Dick is short for Richard."

The man on the porch busts out laughing. "Paul. Paul Yokum. I probably should have introduced myself. But that is clever. Most call me worse than that."

Christian chuckles. "Ask Mister Carver. He knows what we found."

CHAPTER SIXTEEN

Couldn't Miss This One After All

Myles

Oh shit.

Christian left, closing the door behind him. The table was cleared, food put away, dishes washed.

The whole living room is waiting for me to explain what his parting shot was. Dean is snuggled in Blanche's arms. He must have picked up on the tension, wanting his momma the moment he saw her and won't leave her arms now.

I owe the woman looking at me from my recliner an explanation. With a deep breath, I kneel down in front of her. Might as well get on my knees in case I need to beg for forgiveness.

"When Dean was born, I came back to the hospital to check on you guys. I thought it was odd that you named him Dean, you had been saying that you were naming him Aaron when asked. I overheard you telling the nurse that his name was Dean because it was my middle name and I was there when he was born."

She nods and pushes the floor with her toes as Dean snuffles in her arms, soothing him.

"I didn't know how you knew my middle name, I later remembered Grams saying my full name at your baby shower." I look over at the woman who is back in the rocker. She smirks at me because she said it for fondling Blanche's boobs. I did a lot more than that later that night. "What you don't know is that when I came back, they had just come out of your room and having you fill out papers. The nurse laid down the tablet you had just completed the birth certificate with on the station and then got called away to another room. I picked it up, backed up a couple pages, filled in the father section and submitted it."

Blanche is just staring at me. I need her to say something. I glance around the room. Everyone has varying looks of shock on their faces. Might as well get it all out. I pull my phone from my pocket. I'd been taking pictures all night like everyone else so had it on me when I normally leave it on the counter near my keys. Tapping the home screen of the photo of us I took that night of the baby shower, I open the app and hand it to Blanche. There is a blip over her house because she left her phone there to charge when we picked up Dean and Lance.

"Is that? Are you tracking me? Is that what you and Grams were talking about." She pinches and spreads her fingers on the screen to zoom in.

I nod, waiting for her to say more.

"Why? For how long?"

Mom says my name behind me with that warning tone that tells me I need to keep the wooden spoons from her. "Since New Year's. Because I needed to know you were safe and until I could figure out how to make you mine, I needed to do it this way. I even made sure your car was always cleared of snow before the end of your day at school. I won't be removing it, because well, because. But I will turn it on for you, so you can see me too. I think I worked out how, who, is making it glitch occasionally."

"Stalker." Dylan starts to snicker but the sound of head slap comes from behind me. "Owww. Moooom, Marley hit me."

Blanche snorts and then covers her mouth. She looks at the ceiling to get herself under control. "Ok, so I get wanting to keep me safe. I understand that it would be hard to do since we weren't a couple, family. Creepy, but understandable. I get how you work when it comes to the people you care about. I really appreciate the snow shoveling, I did think it was Dad though. I'm not sure how I feel about Dean's birth certificate. I haven't even got it or his social security card yet, so that is why I haven't noticed it. How were you going to explain it when I got them?"

I reach for the book on the table next to my chair. I'm a bit of a closet nerd and was reading the Supernatural series for the fifth time when the mail came a while back. I hand Blanche the two envelopes. They are her name but with my address. I did more than fill in the father section on Dean's paperwork.

She opens them, careful not to disturb the sleeping toddler in her arms. Her eyebrows fly up when she sees what else I did. I'm not sure if the sleeping boy is going to keep me safe. I can't read her face as she looks at both pieces of paper. "Dean Lance... Carver."

There is a scuffle behind me, looking over my shoulder, I see Pops and Dylan holding Mom back. I'm a little scared of what she might do if she gets loose before Blanche forgives me.

I turn back to Blanche, knee walking closer to her. "Blanche? Sweets? We can change it back. I'll pay for it. I'm sorry."

She keeps looking at the papers, silent tears slipping down her cheeks.

"You know what, I'm not sorry. I might have fucked up, but I'm not sorry."

"Language." Several voices reprimand me from the room that is waiting to see what Blanche does.

"Tell me what to do. Do you need me to leave? Take you home? I'll do it. I won't like it. I meant it when I said you're mine. Dean's mine. That I wanted you both from the beginning."

"One more thing. When Richard, Paul, came to serve me the first time, you weren't there when my world began crumbling. Where did you go? Why did you leave me?" I need this other thing cleared up. The final thing that has been bothering me.

Myles rubs my knee, pressing into my legs to get as close to me as possible. "I went after him. I wanted to know what was going on. The first time I confronted him, he was there to serve papers. The second time I saw him, he told me he was ordered to investigate and report. I ordered him to show me everything before he submitted it. He found nothing that showed you in a bad light, nothing that they could hold against you, I made sure of it. I handled it, protected you the way I thought you needed. I'm not saying I'm sorry, I'm not. But I promise to get better at talking to you. To inform you of what I'm doing and why."

With a deep breath, Blanche lays the papers on the arm of the chair. Dean's birth certificate and social security card both clearly say Dean Lance Carver. I love seeing my name with his and soon, his mother will have it too. "I might be stupid, but I'm not mad. This just goes to show that what you said is true. That you want us. We need to talk about how you know the Davies threatened me," he gives a single nod," just, no more sneaky shit. And I might be mad later, but these damn hormones have me wanting to kiss you and say shit like 'aww, you love me'."

Dylan

My brother low-key stalks a woman, tampers with the birth registration of her son to claim him as his, I now know he broke into my office and read her file, knocks her up even if not on purpose, regardless of rumors being spread by another woman, and gets said girl.

We will take care of the rumors and the one spreading them later.

The lawyer in me wants to say he needs to be behind bars. The brother wants to make fun of him. The man wants to clap him on the shoulder and say good job. The jealous monster wants to do it myself.

Keeley is walking back up from the barn with an empty container in her hand. I saw her out the window taking the leftovers that weren't savable out to the cats at Mom's insistence and stepped out to keep an eye on her. The path may be clear but is so packed with snow it can be slick.

"Ewww. I knew you were disgusting after you spit half chewed food on my plate but that is just gross." She stops on the path below from where I'm leaning on the porch support at the top of the back steps.

"There are worse habits I could have." I take the final drag on the thin cigar between my fingers before dropping the butt in the mason jar on the rail. "And my sister whacked that food out of me because I was choking. You know, saved my life? Something I noticed you didn't even attempt to help with."

Now that the cigarillo is out and the smoke has dissipated, Keeley comes up the steps with a small cough. Fuck, I forgot she is allergic, I just needed a bit of something to take off the edge after Christian's appearance. Alcohol is too tempting to get lost in, especially after all those years of working for Robert Luske. Wrinkling her nose, Keeley steps past me with a shiver.

I'm just noticing her choice of clothing as she decided to go out into nineteen degree weather. Her pajamas were discarded after brunch in favor of some thermal pants and top with a flannel over them. Her boots aren't tied, the laces wet and flapping from being walked on. The whole ensemble is black but for the green squares on her button up shirt. Her long gray hair which is sporting some tinsel looking strands in red and green for the holidays is in two braids over her shoulders.

The small smattering of stars with a moon drawn next to her left eye looks like they might be becoming permanent. She tests locations and designs before committing to them, smart but I wish she wouldn't feel the need to mark herself up as a healing mechanism. I overheard her tell someone once it was cheaper than therapy. It was said in a joking tone but I could see she meant it. It hurts that I might be the reason she needs some of that healing. I'm not conceited to think I'm the whole reason she might need therapy, but I will own the shit I did that might have contributed to it.

"Where's your coat? You know better than to go out like that."

Sniffing at my comment, she goes to move past me and back into the warmth beckoning from the windows. "I wasn't intending to be out here long but some jackass decided he needed to stop me to talk. You know what is wrong with you?"

I can't take another word. She is going to say something smart, piss me off and we will be at each other again. I grab

160

her, pulling her into my arms and coat I didn't zip, giving her some warmth.

Keeley

What the ever loving fuck?!

The warmth coming off Dylan is nice as I was standing there freezing my ass off. Anger is not a substitute for true warmth. I can smell the cigar thing he just put out on him. It isn't as unpleasant as cigarettes are, but I'm allergic to all burnt tobacco. If I was to get too close, for too long, I'd need my inhaler and a dose of allergy medication. I don't fancy a benadryl induced nap, so I waited until he was finished smoking before coming back up from loving on the trio of cats that call this place home.

Another thing I'm allergic to. The list is long.

My brain and tongue come unstuck at the same time. "What are you doing?"

Dylan glances up and my eyes follow. "Mistletoe."

Once upon a time, I would have had an entire moment at being in Dylan's arms, him about to kiss me. But that was a lifetime ago. He turned out to be no better than the other bros that ran with Bryce and continued his manwhore ways after high school, just not on the level that Bryce did. The man never takes a woman out past five dates, doesn't do long term.

He may have led the charge that saved Brandon that day too, but I can't let myself be sucked into the orbit of a man that could have helped instead of feeding the fires that made me and my best friend pariahs. Flames that have me a mid-twenty something virgin because I can't trust a man long enough to let my guard down.

Placing my hands on his chest and pushing as his face lowers to mine, I freeze Dylan where he stands with three words, "I'm seeing someone."

Review

OVERALL ☆☆☆☆☆

SPICE 🌶🌶🌶🌶🌶

WRITING 🖊🖊🖊🖊🖊

CHARACTERS 👤👤👤👤👤

ENDING ♡♡♡♡♡
*EVEN IF A CLIFFHANGER

NOTES, PAGES, REVIEW

ABOUT S.L. SIMMONS

The wilds of Appalachia are not big enough to contain the mind that is S.L. Simmons. Instead, she dreams up places where her characters can live out their own happily ever afters because she is living hers.

If you want to know the story of how she and her husband came to be together, feel free to ask. It reads like a missed chance/lost love/reunited trope that will have you saying, 'that would make a good book'. Yes, she is married to a real life *guy from the book*.

It all started with a song that would not leave her alone resulting in a story writing itself in her head before ever seeing the light of day. The voices have multiplied and so have the books. Don't be quick to pigeonhole her into a genre or trope though. She has several works in progress that differ from her breakout series of Mistletoe Fails. Contemporary holiday to paranormal to alien peen, she has a whole brain of stories to tell.

With an OCD and ADD brain fueled by caramel mochaccinos, the space around her protected by a pack of doggos, she writes out the stories that pop into her head at random times.

WHERE TO FIND HER

The best way to keep up with S.L. Simmons is on her website
www.slsimmonswordsmith.com

Blog, calendar of events, merchandise; all there and more.

www.ingramcontent.com/pod-product-compliance
Lightning Source LLC
Chambersburg PA
CBHW071516170626
46811CB00007B/2875